DAWSON

JASPER SPRINGS

BOOK TWO

BY EVIE RILEY

Dawson

An MM Enemies To Lovers Romance

Jasper Springs

Book Two

DAWSON

**Things are heating up in
Jasper Springs...**

Dawson Richards is Jasper Springs's very own famed "Mr. March." Rescuing people—and cats—is what the hunky firefighter does best. That is, when his infuriating nemesis isn't throwing a monkey wrench into Dawson's hard work.

Claims Adjuster Nolan Harding moved to Jasper Springs seeking a fresh start, but after months of working with an annoying but sinfully delicious fireman who drives him crazy, Nolan is nearing the end of his rope.

When a fire hits home for Dawson, he and Nolan must work together to close the case correctly and on time.

Can they put aside their grievances and their undeniable attraction to get the job done? Or will the heat consume their hearts too?

Readers seeking an enemies to lovers romance set in a cozy little town may find this story checks those boxes. While Dawson and Nolan may have cameos in future stories, each book in this series can be read as a standalone.

CHAPTER ONE

Dawson

"BINGO!" NOLAN SCREAMED, his shrill voice nearly exploding my eardrums even though he was at least three tables away.

Instinctively, my jaw tensed, his excitement like nails on a damn chalkboard.

"Fucking hell, I was one away from winning!" I groaned, ripping the sliver of thin bingo paper in half.

"Spend all your stripper money from the calendar so soon?" Cade ribbed me, his new boyfriend, Weston, shaking his head. He was still red in the face from the last round of karaoke.

"You're not supposed to show the

firehose upfront, you know. That's what OnlyFans is for," Weston jabbed, flashing a cocky grin.

I rolled my eyes.

"No, and fuck you," I said sarcastically, throwing Mitch, Cade, and Weston into a fit of laughter.

"Sore loser," Cade said as he drained the last of his beer.

I watched in disdain as Nolan fucking Harding stumbled up to the stage, like a deer who'd been hit by a car.

What the hell has him out of his office this late, anyway?

He had the audacity to shove his black, nerdy glasses up his nose just a hair before grabbing his winnings, the light of the stage shining on him like some damn halo.

But Nolan was far from an angel.

He was, in fact, the kryptonite to my Superman, the Joker to my Batman.

He was my arch nemesis.

I watched him with a scathing look as Miguel handed him his winnings, his smile stirring some sort of hurricane inside of me.

Those pouty lips, that perfect jawline...

The thought of those lips wrapped

around my cock until I'd face fucked the glasses right off his pretty face had fueled more of my fantasies than I cared to admit, but who wasn't prone to a hate-fuck fantasy every now and then? It didn't mean I *liked* the guy.

I most certainly didn't like him, and the desire to make his life a living hell was only equal to my need to run.

Run away from this damn disaster of a night.

At that moment, Nolan looked up directly at me, catching my gaze. I didn't miss the blush that spread across his nose, continuing on to his cheeks. The sight immediately caused my brain to spur those hate-fuck fantasies at the wrong time, causing my damn cock to twitch. I grunted in response, breaking his gaze, feeling hot all of a sudden.

"Fuck this, I'm out," I said as I pushed away from the table, leaving Mitch to browse his phone while Weston and Cade made out like two teenagers on prom night.

Mitchell waved a hand in the air, not looking up from his phone. "Toodles, Mr. March," he said dryly.

"Nice meeting you, Dawson," Weston

said politely, between breaths. "Officially, I mean."

I waved him off with a half-smile, but he'd gone back to playing tonsil hockey with Cade.

I made my way toward the bar to pay my tab, feeling only slightly buzzed. Max saw me coming a mile away, reaching over a group of patrons to hand me my check, which I quickly paid.

"Thanks, Max," I said as I stumbled over some douchebag's big ass feet that were sticking out.

"Watch where you're going, asshole," Bigfoot spoke, turning to me with an angry expression.

"Keep all hands, arms, legs, and feet inside the airplane, asshole, and I won't have to," I nipped. Max shot me a scathing look as the man sweetly told me just where to shove his gigantic foot.

"You wish," I drawled, feeling more than irritated.

The night had been a bust. I was off my game.

I'd had a shit day at work, dealing with fucking Nolan again, questioning one of my recent claims for damages, my inbox starting to fill up at that point. Why the twat felt the need to question ninety percent of my claims was beyond me.

I had sincerely fucked up everything else in my life, but the firehouse was the one place I knew my shit. At least, I had until Nolan showed up two years ago after my ex left my ass high and dry to chase his financial dreams.

One of these days, I was going to fucking ruin Nolan for being an eternal pain in the ass.

I slapped some extra bills down on the counter for Max's tip as I turned away, charismatically flipping off Bigfoot in the process.

"Sayonara, assholes," I hollered over the chatter, heading through the bar to the shadowed corridor toward the side exit.

I knew most people didn't use it, because it was technically an emergency exit, but I didn't much care at the moment, and Max or Miguel would not stop me. Fire exits were second nature to me. I pulled my phone out of my back pocket, deciding I should probably queue up a ride, knocking into another asshole, who *stepped* on me.

"What the fuck, watch where you're—"

My entire body flared with heat when I laid eyes on the culprit blocking my exit.

"Perhaps your vision needs to be checked, *Dawson,* because lord knows if I was a snake I would have bitten you," Nolan snapped as he adjusted his crooked glasses like he was *soooo much smarter* than me.

Instinctively, I bit back, "Ain't nothing wrong with my vision, Harding. Not my fault your spineless ass blends into the fucking shadows."

Nolan had the audacity to *scoff* at me, like I was the one ruining his life.

"Besides, we both know your bite is about as hard as a toothless alligator."

Nolan scowled at me, crossing his arms as the bar lights shifted, casting stray green and blue lights our way. In the beams of colored light, I could see some slight definition in his biceps from the way his short sleeves cut against his skin.

Huh, that's new.

"You think you know me, huh? I got news for you, Dawson. You don't. You don't know what I'm capable of." Nolan's voice was full of false bravado, edged with something else I'd never heard before.

Something that made my blood heat and my cock twitch as his brown eyes roved over me before settling on my lips.

Was Nolan... was he *flirting* with me?

Maybe I'm more buzzed than I thought. Yeah, Uber is a definite.

I took a step closer to Nolan, backing him up against the wall next to the exit.

"Oh, I think I know what you're capable of. You're capable of being a giant pain in my fucking ass."

The thud of Nolan's back hitting the wall sounded as I leaned in closer. I held his fiery gaze, before I nipped my teeth at him, expecting him to jump like a scared dog, but instead, he only leaned in closer.

So close, I could feel the heat of his words on my skin, smell the sweet faint scent of lime and tequila on his breath.

And then the strangest thing happened. Nolan fucking *whimpered.*

Like some damsel in distress.

Like prey.

I snickered even as the sight of his tongue flicking out to moisten his lips caused my cock to twitch.

"Just what I thought. Snakes don't have backbones," I hissed. Then I saw something shift in his eyes, his shoulders tensing as he pushed into my space, his own lips pulled back in a snarl in retaliation.

"Maybe not, but their jaws can eat predators twice their size," Nolan answered, his deep breath full of snark like a petulant little brat.

"Is that what you want, Harding? To eat a predator twice your size?"

My head spun as my cock twitched and perked up, my entire being running on instinct.

Nolan pushed at my chest lightly with one finger, pushing me back.

"Wouldn't be the first time," he said, his voice filled with attitude as I stumbled backward.

His words fell on me like a heavy steel beam.

The unmistakable realization hit me. I'd never assumed Nolan was into guys. Hell, I'd assumed from his lack of conversation about anything outside of work and making my life a living hell, he was just another dorky asshole who'd been friend-zoned by all his chick friends, which was why I didn't feel too bad about dreaming about stuffing his mouth full with my dick as punishment during happy time.

My cock *throbbed* with interest. Clearly, it had a mind of its own.

My phone had the audacity to break up the wonderfully tense moment by sounding off the incessant rings that told me my ride had arrived.

"Saved by the bell. Lucky you," Nolan quipped, hip checking me as he slid past me, heading back toward the bar, leaving me hard, confused, and in shock.

What the fuck?

CHAPTER TWO

Nolan

WHAT THE FUCK is wrong with me?

I braced my arms against the table, the room spinning as I mentally recounted the absolute meltdown I'd had on my way back from the bathroom.

Of all the people to run into, to be here in this damn bar tonight, of all nights...

I just *had* to run into the one firefighter who I'd been stupidly fantasizing about since I ended up assigned to this region.

As if moving to a new city wasn't hard enough, it became quite clear, quite fast, that I did not fit in. Not at the office, and certainly not at the firehouse that my firm worked with. Not that I fit in... well, anywhere really.

My mama used to say I was just "shy", but I'm not shy. I'm awkward. Sheldon Cooper's got nothing on me.

In my head, everything makes sense. I can say what I want, dreaming up scenarios where I blend in naturally, cool as a cucumber and the life of the party.

Where I can pretend I'm someone like Dawson Richards.

Bold, confidant. Sexy enough to be practically naked on a calendar that I jack off to after a long, boring day of numbers and figures.

Which is probably how I would have spent my twenty-eighth birthday, had my best friend Allie not convinced me to go out for once. To "let loose and have a little fun." Even if I would be doing it alone, like I had for the last couple of years since moving here. It wasn't like I hadn't *tried* to meet people, but the town of Jasper Springs wasn't really all that different from where I grew up. No one took a second glance at me. No one except Mr. March. At least when I first arrived.

Dawson seemed cool. All charisma and perfect smiles, that natural flirtatious air about him that was some cross between a used car salesman and high school prom king.

I thought maybe he was different. Maybe, just maybe, moving here wouldn't be so bad if I could make one friend.

But all thoughts of hope and happiness diminished when work called us both, and Dawson's short attention span rendered me forgotten.

Until I'd been called out on my first claim, which happened to be a local fire that Dawson had responded to.

I tried to remain professional, because what else could I do?

I'd been promoted to Jasper Springs for a reason, and that reason was there were far too many claims and not enough people to accurately investigate and close the cases. I'd always been good at my job, meeting my quotas and then some. But I'd never dreamed that I would be fought quite this hard on them by one stubborn firefighter.

Who just had you backed up against the wall like some villain from a comic book.

The memory of Dawson's piercing gaze, the way he lumbered over me, caused my cock to stiffen like a lightning rod.

It wasn't like I hadn't thought about a scenario like that before. In fact, it was one I thought about often.

It was like some other entity had possessed me, because the minute my back hit the wall, some switch inside of me flipped.

His hot breath on me, his six foot one frame towering over my measly five foot eight inches...

The command in his voice, the way his eyes blazed as his gaze fell to my lips, causing my stomach to twist into knots.

In the presence of Dawson Richards, I was someone else, and I wasn't sure how I felt about that.

I decided that I'd had enough of all this birthday insanity and threw down some money, feeling like I needed to get as far away from M's place and the memory of Dawson and his ridiculously hot stare as I could get.

But it was no use.

I closed the door, feeling even more defeated as the lights came on to illuminate my empty apartment.

I flipped the lock, tossing my keys on the kitchen counter as I opened my fridge to pull out the oversized cupcake Allie had delivered to the office earlier. I meticulously peeled the blue wrapper back, section by section to keep the confectionery delicacy from crumbling.

"Happy birthday to me," I sighed out, feeling exhaustion kick in. I devoured the chocolate cake in less than three bites, but it did nothing to sate the emptiness I felt in my stomach.

After I'd eaten my cupcake of shame, I removed my clothes, tossing them into the wicker hamper in the hallway, relishing in the cool air of my apartment as it hit my sensitive skin. I always kept the place at sixty-eight degrees.

As I crawled into bed, my mind wandered to thoughts of darkened hallways, of a tall, sexy man who made my insides twist and my cock spring to life. I groaned as I looked at the digital clock on my nightstand. 11:30pm.

Twenty-eight years old, single, and in bed by eleven thirty. Yeah, talk about lame.

There was no chance in hell anyone would find routine and order sexy.

I closed my eyes as I let my hand slide beneath the waistband of my boxers, wrapping my fist around the head of my cock. My thumb brushed over the tip, feeling the faint beginnings of precum coat my fingertips. Slowly, I tugged at the sensitive skin, building a steady rhythm as I let my mind wander further down the darkened corridor of fantasy, to thoughts of copper eyes and broad shoulders, to fists slammed against the wall beside my head.

Of thick fingers around my neck, and fiery lips that cursed me to high hell before they claimed mine.

Of the weight of his body on top of me as he fucking *owned me.*

The thought of his cock sliding against mine, pressed against the wall, hard and wet, threw me over the edge.

I cupped my hand over my swollen head as I came, groaning in defeat as my cock pulsed, sticky, warm wetness spreading through my fingers as I fought to catch my breath. I wished it wasn't mine.

"Holy fuck." I sighed, staring up at the ceiling as I fell back to earth.

I knew then, as I lay there, that Dawson Richards was going to be the fucking death of me.

CHAPTER THREE

Dawson

THE WHOLE RIDE home all I could think about was Nolan. Which only irritated me. His snippy little comments, his blush on stage, the way he fucking *whimpered* and leaned into me...

Fuck.

I hated it. I hated that he pushed my buttons so easily.

Or that he is capable of pushing my buttons at all.

I angrily threw my keys down in the bowl after locking the door, knowing there was only one way to truly work out my frustrations.

It didn't take long for me to settle in on

my couch, pulling up my favorite go-to porn. I let the video play while I got comfortable, letting my cock spring free from my pants as I slid out of them. Leaning back against the soft cushions, I gave myself a good smack, watching my cock bounce with vibrancy as I focused on the video in front of me, specifically the way Mr. Big Cock was pounding himself into the tight little ass of the moaning computer nerd in front of him.

"You like that don't you, you little slut?" Mr. Big Cock drawled, shoving his subject's head down into the dirt.

"Yes..." I groaned along with him as I gripped my own rigid rod, closing my eyes. The sound of Mr. Big Cock's wet, slick cock and his nerdy little slut's moans as he begged for Mr. Big Cock covered me like a blanket, making my own dick throb, eliciting a deep groan from me as I let my mind fill in the blanks.

Smooth, round, pale cheeks that I could watch my thick cock disappear into formed in my brain, the image of my fingers tangled in dark locks as I gripped tightly, yanking them to turn and look at me over their shoulder.

DAWSON

Deep brown eyes met mine. Nolan stared at me over his glasses, throaty moans escaping his lips as his tight ass clenched me, and I immediately opened my eyes, ceasing my hold on my cock, my thumb sliding through the steady amount of precum that had already collected at the tip.

"Fuck!" I hissed as my cock throbbed and I tried to catch my breath. My gaze diverted back to the television just in time to see Mr. Big Cock quickening his pace. My hips involuntarily thrust into my still hand, clearly not getting the message.

"I don't know how much more I can take," Computer Cum Slut cried, his arm muscles tightening, his voice shaking. "Please..."

I leaned my head back once more, a sheen of sweat breaking out as I closed my eyes. In the darkness, Nolan stared at me, begging me like Computer Cum Slut.

My cock *throbbed* in my hand and I squeezed it tightly, spreading the warm, sticky precum along my shaft as I picked up my pace again.

I needed to come so fucking bad, and I didn't want to edge myself after the fucking day I'd had.

So I figured, why the hell not. It's not like I hadn't fantasized about Nolan before. It didn't mean anything.

At least that's what I told myself as I let his image fill my brain, as I allowed myself to fantasize about driving my aching cock in Nolan's tight little ass while he begged me to fuck him faster, harder.

"That's it, come for Daddy," Mr. Big Cock grunted from my speakers.

And I did.

I came like a fucking geyser, with a frustrated growl. "Fuck!"

I don't know how long I stayed there, frozen with my hand on my weeping cock, but it felt like forever.

When I finally opened my eyes to survey the mess I'd made, I felt awash with a mix of emotions.

Shame.

Embarrassment.

Desire.

Guilt.

Sadness.

I couldn't remember coming that hard *ever.* Which is why I knew I needed to do whatever I could to forget what had just happened.

DAWSON

You've got to get a hold of yourself, Dawson. You've got to forget tonight, forget Nolan altogether.

And as I regrettably stopped the video, and I cleaned myself of what may have been the equivalent of the Guinness World Record's largest load ever, I promised myself I'd do just that.

I would forget Nolan Harding and his stupid, pretty face and whimper, his blush, his soulful brown eyes and nerdy glasses.

But first, I was going to make him pay for ruining my fucking life.

CHAPTER FOUR

Nolan

I'D JUST GOTTEN out of a meeting with my regional boss when I entered my office and saw I had several missed calls, all from the same number.

The Jasper Springs VFD.

I sighed as I plopped down in my ergonomic chair and just as I set to pick up the phone, it rang again, JSVFD appearing on my phone screen again.

I picked up the phone. "Nolan Harding, Breisinger Insurance,"

"Where the fuck have you been?" Dawson snapped on the other end, immediately throwing me a curveball.

I mean, I had a feeling it was him who

called, but there was no way to be sure.

I pulled up my email, noting he'd already sent me two emails today, and I wasn't even halfway through my shift.

What's up his ass today?

"Doing my job, Mr. Richards. Something you clearly don't understand."

"Don't get cute with me, *Mr. Harding.*"

Why his bite and the way he said my name made me blush, I didn't know, but I was thankful that I was alone, in my office, away from prying eyes.

Which also meant no one else could hear me.

"If I wanted to get cute with you, *Dawson*, I wouldn't be vague about it. Lord knows you need everything spelled out for you."

"Fuck you, Nolan."

"I see we're past pleasantries now. Is there a reason for your call, or did you just want to hear my *cute* voice?" I said.

What the fuck?

Where did that come from?

There was a pause, the only sound Dawson's breathing on the other end, which strangely caused my cock to twitch. I adjusted myself in my pants, letting out a frustrated sigh.

What was his deal?

Before I could tell him I didn't have time to deal with his bullshit because I had a thousand emails to answer and claims to investigate, he spoke.

"I submitted a claim for Jonathan Bradish two days ago and no one's even been out to the guy's house yet to check anything."

What?

Since when did Dawson keep tabs on my job?

Naturally, the shift in conversation made me defensive. Contrary to Dawson's belief that I did nothing but sit around on my ass and jack off all day, I had a laundry list of claims to investigate as well as a boatload of administrative tasks and meetings seeing as I was practically one promotion away from becoming the manager of this damn branch.

"I'm aware of my own case load, Dawson. I don't need you to tell me how to do my job."

"Then do *your* fucking job, Nolan. Or I'll do it for you," he said gruffly, his tone all commanding and... *hot.*

Fuck, why does he sound so hot when he's pissed off?

My cock agreed as it twitched in my pants again. I crossed my legs only to apply pressure, because I did *not* have time in my schedule to take care of an inappropriate erection.

And the object of my fantasies chastising me like a bad child, is definitely not helping matters.

I pulled up my case file for Jonathan Bradish, noting that the property wasn't all that far from the office. Glancing at the clock, I knew I'd have to go to lunch soon, but maybe, just maybe I'd be able to squeeze in a trip.

I knew I should have been honest, professional, and that I should have just told Dawson I'd take care of it.

But a part of me *liked* hearing him all worked up, liked pushing his buttons... and my cock certainly liked it.

Liked *him.*

So instead of doing what I should have done, I did the exact opposite.

I took Dawson's bait like a famished fish.

"You know, *Dawson,* you catch more flies with honey than you do with vinegar," I drawled as I swiveled in my chair, licking my lips.

"What the fuck is that supposed to mean?" Dawson griped. His reaction caused a grin to spread across my face.

He really made it so easy sometimes. He was like a whistling teapot. Let him steam long enough and he'd boil over.

"It means that if you want something out of me, you're going to have to ask me. Nicely."

"Oh, I'll give you *nice*, Harding. I'll give you a nice, swift kick in that tight ass of yours, set you in the right direction."

His words caused my cock to throb, and I could already feel a wet spot forming in my underwear.

Fuuuuuck, why is this so hot?

Wait, did he just call my ass...

"I'm waiting, Dawson," I said, my breath coming out much heavier than it should have been as I tried to stifle how fucking turned on I was at the moment.

So unprofessional.

God, what is wrong with me?

I closed my eyes as I tried to regain my sanity.

"Nolan," he breathed my name like it was a sin. Another pause, Dawson's heavy breathing in my ear hovering like some sort of spell.

"Would you *please* do me a favor?" Dawson spoke with command, but his entire tone had shifted from demanding and angry to something else.

Smooth, sexy.

Like pure silk.

My entire body loosened, and I wanted to *melt* into the sound of his voice. I could imagine him telling me to get on my knees with a voice like that, which was also not helping my current situation.

I'd never heard him speak like *that* to anyone.

"Yes, Dawson?" I said, licking my lips, stilling my voice.

"Would you *please* be a good little pencil pusher and do your fucking job so I can do mine? Thanks, sweetheart. You're a doll," he said before he hung up, leaving me breathless, with a raging hard on at eleven thirty in the morning.

The dial tone echoed in my ears as I opened my eyes, staring at the ceiling.

What the fuck just happened?

Just as I hung up the phone, my cell phone went off.

I'm never getting any work done today.

I pulled out my cell, knowing without bothering to look who was calling. Very few people actually had my cell phone number, on account because I didn't have many friends.

But I'd also set Allie's ringtone to *All The Single Ladies*, which she insisted was the best song ever made.

Well, that's one way to kill a boner.

I punched the green button and answered the call. "Hey, Allie," I said, letting out a deep breath.

"What's wrong? You sound stressed," she said immediately.

I leaned back in my chair, letting the springy bounce soothe my frustration.

"I just got off the phone with Dawson. He called about a case and I just... I guess let him get to me."

"He's such an asshole. Seriously."

"I know, but—"

That's why I like him. I like his shitty attitude, his foul mouth, and he isn't bad on the eyes either...

"I wanted to let you know that I got some time coming up I have to take, so I was thinking maybe I could come visit? Spend the weekend? Get your ass out of the house for a bit?"

I sighed. I wanted to spend time with Allie, I really did, but the last month I'd gotten swamped with work, and I knew I needed to make a dent in my workload.

"Work has been a little nuts as of late, Allie. I'm sorry, I—"

"It's fine, Nolan. I know you're working your ass off right now for that promotion. Just... remember your life doesn't have to be all work, you know."

Her words settled on me, making me feel a mixture of shame, guilt, and loneliness.

It was easy for people like Allie to say that, when they had lives outside of their jobs.

My life *was* my job. It was all I had, because I was alone.

I glanced at the clock, noting it was now nearing quarter to twelve. If I wanted to hit Jonathan Bradish's house, I'd need to get a move on it.

"I like my job..." I said with a whine.

"Mhmmm. I think you just like being around all those sweaty, hot firefighters all day."

Maybe just one hot firefighter.

"I do not—"

"Especially... who is it? Mr. March?" She giggled. "I mean, hell, I'd become a workaholic too for those calendar boys."

She whistled on the other end, throwing me into another blush.

"It's not like that, and you know it. I gotta go though. I have to actually go check out a claim... that's what Dawson called about."

"I'd love to meet the asshole who gets you all flustered someday. Maybe on the next trip you can bring me down to the firehouse and show me what I'm missing," she said sweetly.

"Deal," I promised, and I let her go, getting up from my chair and grabbing my keys.

CHAPTER FIVE

Dawson

I'D JUST MADE it back to the firehouse when my brother called.

"Jonathan, is everything okay?" I asked, my adrenaline still spiked from the shed fire we'd just put out across town in Deer Park.

"Yeah, everything's good, I, uh... you said to give you a call whenever one of the insurance guys showed up, so I just wanted to let you know one of them showed up."

I breathed a sigh of relief. It seemed my lighting a fire under Nolan's ass worked.

"Good. I'll be there in a bit, just getting

out of my gear. Don't let them leave until I get there, okay? I don't want these idiots fucking shit up on my watch."

"Dawson..." my brother protested, but I refused to let him blow me off. It was my job as his big brother to make sure he was okay, and that those asshole adjusters made sure he was covered for his losses. I knew firsthand how they could be sticklers, having dated one of them, especially when it came to folks like my brother who operated their businesses out of their homes.

"I'll see you in a few," I said as I hung up, not giving him a chance to rebuke me.

I didn't bother hitting the showers; instead, I just hung my shit up in my locker and grabbed my keys to my truck. Thankfully, my brother's place was about fifteen minutes away, but with my skilled emergency driving, I could shave off at least five minutes.

Which is exactly what I did.

All the agents at Breisinger drove the same car, a little silver sedan with a big ass logo on the side. It stood out like a sore thumb everywhere, and it was no different parked in front of my brother's house.

DAWSON

From the street, you would have never been able to tell there'd been a fire, but around the back was another story. I parked my truck, hopping out with haste as I entered through the front door. I didn't need to knock, after all, we were family and I was more than expected.

My brother looked up at me from his couch, the agent turning to face me as well...

And when my eyes met surprised brown irises, I think my blood actually boiled. Nolan's eyes widened, his eyebrows shooting up like I'd just caught him with his hand in the cookie jar.

"Dawson, what..." he said as he stood up, my brother following suit.

"Afternoon, Harding," I said as I sauntered past him toward my brother, casting him one of my patented *Mr. March* smiles, if only to appear *nice*.

Truth be told, my adrenaline was still pumping and the sight of those surprised peepers and pouty lips was doing things to me that I didn't want to focus on at the moment.

For starters, my brother was standing next to Nolan... which shouldn't have bothered me as much as it did.

But it did.

"I told you, Dawson, I have it covered here..." Jonathan protested with a sigh, sliding his hands into his jean pockets. He stared at me with an annoyed expression.

"Nonsense, this is my job, Jon. I told you..."

"Isn't there like a cat in a tree somewhere that requires your attention?" Nolan said, shaking off his surprise.

Jonathan laughed. "I take it you two know one another pretty well?"

I took a step closer to Nolan, using my frame to loom ominously over him.

At least, I hoped I looked ominous and not like a stiff giraffe.

"Yeah, Harding and I are the best of buds. Aren't we, *Nolan?*" I said with a smirk.

"Uh..." I didn't miss the way Nolan's gaze dipped to my lips, or the blush forming across his nose, spreading into his cheeks. The sight made my cock twitch, and I shoved my hand in my pocket, if only to adjust myself.

I needed to remember where I was, and what I was actually supposed to be doing here...

"Sure. We'll go with that," Nolan said, his voice as polite and professional as he could muster. Though clearly I'd caused him some distress as his gaze roved over me from head to toe.

"Seriously, I got it handled. But if you are going to stay until Nolan leaves, at least take a shower. You look like hell."

"Well, that would be because I came straight here from a fire, because I didn't want to miss busting the balls of your claims adjuster," I said with a grin.

Nolan shook off whatever it was that had him flustered as he crossed his arms. "I could report you for harassment, you know," he said in a hushed voice, raising a brow.

I leaned closer by an inch, licking my lips. He made it so easy sometimes.

"But you won't, because you're a good little pencil pusher aren't you, Nolan?" I said as I stepped back, removing my shirt.

I didn't miss how his eyes widened, how his mouth dropped open in stunned annoyance, or how he gazed back at me with a fire that had nothing to do with the one we were both here about.

And seeing his eyes ablaze like that caused my cock to stiffen, and I knew I needed to get away from there before I really decided to go all in and give him something to report.

"Fine. I could use a cold shower," I said out loud for everyone to hear as I headed for the hallway bathroom, leaving Nolan and my brother to the situation at hand.

Once the door was locked, I let out a frustrated sigh as I took the rest of my clothes off, folding them neatly and setting them on the back of the toilet.

I wasn't lying about needing a cold shower, as once I was alone, and my cock was free, it could have passed as a compass with how north it was pointing.

I huffed a sigh of annoyance as I stepped in the shower, hoping the cool water would help put out the fire that had started to build inside of me from just the sight of Nolan on my brother's couch.

Images flashed in my mind that I knew I shouldn't be thinking about, given current circumstances, but I knew better than to try and fight the fantasy forming in my brain.

I'd seen the way Nolan looked at me, how he blushed and stammered. A part of me liked that I obviously made him nervous, even if it wasn't a sexual thing for him.

I liked that I could get under his skin...

Not to mention our phone call earlier had worked me up into a heat I hadn't quite expected. The last thing I wanted to do was wax one out at the firehouse, when I was on call. It was just a stroke of luck that we'd gotten called out. Well, lucky for me anyway, if only because it gave me something else to focus on other than Nolan fucking Harding.

It was like over the phone, he was someone else. His voice was different, cockier, sexier.

God what is wrong with me?

Am I admitting Nolan is sexy?

Yes, I was. But I rationalized it was easier to separate the fantasies I had about Nolan from the actual person he was.

But when he'd *demanded* that I ask him nicely, his voice taking on that dark, smooth edge, I nearly lost it.

I'd never heard Nolan talk to anyone like that. Hell, I didn't know he was capable of sounding like a phone sex operator. His words from last night rang in my memory.

You don't know what I'm capable of, Dawson.

Apparently, I didn't.

I wrapped my hand around my cock, knowing it was better to ride the wave than to swim against it.

I let my thoughts wander to dark, sexy phone operator voices, imagining putting the little brat in his place, right over the arm of my brother's couch. I imagined driving him over the edge until he apologized for his sudden, cocky new attitude, imagined bringing him right to the edge, until...

My abs clenched as warm cum sprayed out again with a force I wasn't used to.

Fuuuuck.

That was twice now. Twice, that the thought of using Nolan like my own personal cocksleeve had made me come like a damn teenager who just discovered his dick.

I really needed to get a hold of myself. I needed to quit while I was ahead. I pumped the last bits of my release as I caught my breath, swearing that once I left that shower, it would be a clean slate.

And when I had managed to cleanse my skin and my brain, only then did I turn the water off, and find my way back into my jeans so I could join baby brother and the object of my fantasies gone awry.

When I came to the basement, I could see Nolan on his hands and knees shining a little penlight on something in the corner. The angle showcased the roundness of his ass. An ass I didn't mind looking at, especially since it was clear neither of them noticed my arrival.

"This wasn't in the report," Nolan said, and immediately I tensed, readying to jump to the defense for my brother, but before I could speak, before either of them could turn to see me, he sat back on his heels, looking up at my brother with kind eyes.

"But contrary to what your brother thinks, this is why my job's important. I want to make sure we have *all the information* we need to be able to get you the coverage and reimbursement you deserve."

"I appreciate that, really," Jonathan said, sighing, "I just don't want to get reamed over some stupid detail..."

Nolan stood, brushing the dirt off his knees as he looked to one of the bikes in the corner. My old bike, the one Jonathan was fixing for me, specifically. I kept to the shadows, frozen, watching the scene unfold in front of me.

"I'm sure Dawson didn't note it, because he just didn't know. His job is to fight the fire, not the red tape or the damage it leaves. Don't worry, Mr. Bradish. I'll take care of this."

At that moment, I realized that maybe I had been a little... abrasive with Nolan. I'd assumed he questioned my claims because he was a nitpicking ass, never once considering that maybe his nitpicking actually *helped* my ass.

That was the moment a paint can crashed to the ground, falling right on my fucking foot.

"Fucking ay!" I yelped as I jumped back, causing them both to turn in my direction and notice me.

Well there goes my career in the CIA.

"You coming to wreck my garage now, Daw?" Jonathan teased me.

Nolan's demeanor shifted completely.

Gone was the nice, polite and professional man who was confident and caring regarding his knowledge and job. Instead, Nolan was replaced with the shy, quiet man I'd known for the last two years. The one who couldn't even look at me most days.

"Thought maybe I'd get the renovations started early," I said, shaking off the pain as I walked further into the garage.

"W... well, on that note," Nolan said, getting flustered again as he averted his eyes from me, brushing off some invisible dirt. "I should be getting back... my lunch only goes until... twelve thirty," he stammered.

Jonathan nodded. "Thanks again!" he said as he turned to head back toward the house.

I watched Nolan leave, in slow motion, caught between talking to my brother and apologizing to the man I'd second-guessed.

My lightning rod cock twitched and pointed me in the right direction though.

"Nolan, wait..." I called out, but he was already making a beeline through the garage door toward the side of the street. I hurried to catch him, surprised at how fast he was actually moving. I had to legit sprint to catch him, and when I did, I wrapped my hand around his biceps, stopping him in his tracks. He dug his heels into the grass, coming to a complete stop, almost making me smack right into him.

He looked up at me in surprise. "Dawson..."

His gaze flicked to where my hand wrapped around his arm, and I realized my fingers were *gripping* him rather tightly. I flexed them, letting go, as a wash of nervousness and guilt befell me.

"I just... wanted to apologize," I said, tasting the foreign words on my tongue.

"Apologize for what?" Nolan asked, rubbing his biceps where I'd left a light indentation and a pale red mark.

"I didn't mean to hurt you, I just—"

"It's fine, I promise. You aren't like the Hulk or anything, believe me," he bit.

I wanted to rise to his bait. To fight with him, because his attitude begged for an adjustment as of late, but something told me that wasn't what was best at the moment.

I needed to set the record straight, so I could go on with my day, my life.

Apologize, then everything can go back to normal, and everyone's happy.

"I meant about earlier. On the phone. I was..." I swallowed, trying to find the strength to say the words. It wasn't often I apologized to anyone for anything.

I was a hero, a good guy. Contrary to Nolan's belief, I wasn't an asshole. At least I wasn't an asshole to *everyone*.

Just one person in particular.

"I was a dick, and I shouldn't have bitten your head off. I know you have a job to do, it's just—" I felt strangely flustered as the words poured out of me.

Nolan looked up at me with those same kind eyes he gave my brother, dropping his hand from his biceps. He took a small step closer, his gaze falling to my lips and then back to my eyes again.

"It's just what, Dawson?" he asked in a calm, smooth voice. It wasn't the same smooth and sexy phone operator voice I'd busted a nut to earlier, but it eased something inside of me.

"My brother's all I have, and I just... I just hate not being able to fix this for him. To see him struggle because his shop was his life and now..."

"Hey..." Nolan reached out and set his hand on my arm, his touch soft and warm.

I didn't dislike it. In fact, I wanted to feel his touch all over me, soothing all my worries.

But I figured it was just the adrenaline making me all emotional and weird.

"Everything will be okay, I promise," he said softly. "I'll make sure of it."

I realized somehow we'd gotten closer. Close enough that if I wanted to, I could run my fingers through his dark locks, close enough to kiss.

And that thought was the one that drove me away.

This was not getting back to normal. This was dangerously close to falling over an edge I didn't want to be on.

"I'll hold you to that, Harding," I said gruffly as I headed back to my brother's to grab my shirt I'd left hanging over the edge of his couch, leaving Nolan in my dust once more.

CHAPTER SIX

Nolan

I AM A glutton for punishment.

Clearly, there was no other explanation. I wasn't sure what had gotten into me earlier, except for the fact that Dawson just seemed to be able to draw out parts of me I didn't even know existed.

Flirting with him over the phone was one thing. It was easier to pretend, to channel the person I *wished* I could be when I didn't have to physically look at the man.

I told myself I was going to erase that morning's phone call from my brain completely, and I had every intention of doing so; starting with focusing on work—on the job Dawson was up my ass about—and then he had to show up fresh from a fire, his sandy blond hair all disheveled, his skin flushed and sweaty still, with smudges of ash and soot on his face, with that cocky grin...

Like some hunk out of a romance novel or something.

And then when he *grabbed* me, to apologize... it was like something had shifted in him too, and even though I knew I should have been pissed and I should have told him to back off, and get as far away from me as possible, I found myself falling further into his gravitational pull.

His dark eyes implored mine as his voice cracked just in the slightest, showing off what I gathered was probably the man beneath all the equipment and fireproof armor.

Someone not a lot of people saw, and I couldn't look away. Like a moth, I was drawn to his endearing flame, his change of character, and I couldn't stop myself from falling like a star in his orbit.

His hair was still wet, and he smelled like cedar and spice. I looked up at him through my glasses, my gaze falling over his lips as I wondered for a moment if he would taste as good as he smelled, if his kiss would be as ravaging as the fires he chased, or if it would be a slow burn, like a fine whiskey making its way down your throat.

It had taken nearly all my concentration to fight the desire to take his lips and kiss away the worry that was so evident in his voice and on his face.

But I knew kissing Dawson was both unprofessional and unwarranted.

After all, how could someone like him ever want someone like me?

Even I knew the world wasn't some romance novel. Guys like Dawson could have any man they desired, and guys like me were just the wallflowers in the background, the muted colors of a painting put there only to make brighter ones stand out.

So I did the only thing I could think of. I told him, despite my better judgment, despite the overwhelming desire to kiss him in the yard of his brother's house, that everything was going to be okay, even though I wasn't certain I believed it myself.

At least, where my job was concerned, I meant that promise.

But a part of me was also trying to convince *myself* everything would be okay. That I would walk away and forget that moment, that I'd forget shirtless Dawson standing inches away from me and his spicy scent, his fiery copper eyes, and his sculpted frame, or the way his eyelashes stood out against his tanned skin.

Fucking hell, why do I always do this?

Why do I always fall for beautiful creatures I can never have?

And then it was over, and Dawson walked away, and I let him go like an idiot because I couldn't string my words together and remember how to fucking human.

"Way to go, Nolan," I chastised myself as I started the car. The digital clock blinked to tell me I was perilously close to a late arrival, so I threw my car into gear and sped off for the office, just as my phone rang.

"Harding," I answered the car's bluetooth handsfree, willing my breath to return to normal. I needed to get Dawson Richards out of my head and focus on things that were actually tangible. Like my job, and the promotion that I'd been working toward.

"Oh, Nolan, I'm so glad I got you! I know you're still out on lunch and all, and I was hoping to catch you before you came back…"

I tensed immediately upon hearing my boss Karla's voice. "What's up?" I asked as I steered the car onto Jasper Springs's main street.

I'd always thought the main street here looked like something out of a travel blog or a Hallmark movie. The trees are always the perfect shade of green, the fences always perfectly painted off-white, and the sun lights everything up like Heaven, giving the town an ethereal glow that is somehow both cozy and inspirational.

"Verizon finally showed up to work on the lines, which means we're out of Internet for the next day or so, so you don't need to come back this afternoon," Karla said, trying to hide the excitement in her voice.

Wait…what?

"You mean I—"

"Take the day off, Nolan. I'll call you tomorrow to let you know an update on when it'll be back and when you can come back to the office."

My blood chilled as her words fell on me like heavy stones.

I hadn't taken a day off from work since...

Well, since I moved here pretty much.

Not that I didn't think about it, but what would I do?

It wasn't like I had a group of friends to gallivant around with, not to mention the town itself was pretty sparse in regard to entertainment...

I guess I could go home and maybe go for my daily run a little earlier?

Put a little extra time in?

"Seriously. Go home. Watch some Netflix or something. Take a break for once. I mean it," she said before hanging up, leaving me stunned in silence.

Well, shit.

I casually steered away from the office, slowing my speed now that I knew I didn't have to rush back to work, passing the fire station. When I'd leased my apartment, I'd thought it was a great selling point. Being close to local first responders meant I was in safe hands if something went wrong, but now it was just another reminder that my job was my life.

Instinctually, I looked for Dawson among the crew washing the fire trucks, but he wasn't there. Probably still chatting up his brother about everything.

Must be a slow day.

A part of my brain just couldn't let sleeping dogs lie though, as I tried to picture him among Gina and Sharky, and some of the newer rookies, like Frank. My mind couldn't help but remember a freshly showered and shirtless Dawson looming over me, and of course that was why my brain decided to go spiraling into thoughts of watching him get all wet and soapy, stretching those back muscles as he cleaned the truck, loose suspenders caressing the shape of his ass...

Fuck, now I'm hard.

I groaned in defeat as the light turned green, shifting in my seat to try and quell my burgeoning erection.

The high-pitched tones of Foreigner singing *Hot Blooded* filled the speakers, making me groan all the more. I huffed out a sigh as I pulled into my parking space at Jasper Springs Towers, the apartment complex I'd called home for the last two years. I shifted myself around once more as I exited the car, feeling rather on the spot.

It was pretty early still, and thankfully, that meant there wasn't a lot of traffic, and kids weren't home from school yet, so the complex itself was pretty quiet. Something I appreciated at the time.

I made my way into my apartment, relishing in the privacy of my own home as I attempted to do just what Karla instructed, and take a break.

Which consisted of me trying to get comfortable on my couch as I slipped out of my white shirt and pants down to my boxers while I doomscrolled my tv for something, anything to get my mind off Dawson, that weird phone conversation, or the last twenty four hours, really.

I settled on some older episodes of *Rescue Me*, trying to do exactly as Karla as said and relax. But neither my mind nor my dick seemed to get the memo.

I huffed out a sigh of frustration, rolling my eyes as I leaned back into my couch cushions, knowing there was truly only one way to quiet my thoughts and get on with my day.

I closed my eyes, slid my hand in my

boxers and let my mind wander, to Dawson and his dark, sexy voice over the phone, the memory of his hot, shirtless self standing above me, remembering that spicy cedar scent and those perfect, kissable lips.

Fuck.

I'd barely gotten into my fantasy before I was pulsing with need, aching to be touched. I just wished someone else other than myself could touch me.

My mind wandered to the memory of Dawson's hands on my skin, when he'd grabbed me, filling in the spaces of fantasy as I let my thoughts spiral, imagining those same warm, rough hands wrapped around my cock, squeezing, sliding...

I grunted out a frustrated sound as I came, much too soon for my own liking as ropes of warm, sticky cum coated my shaft and fingers, making me feel a mix of shame, guilt, and relief.

Well at least that's taken care of, now perhaps I can get back to being a functional human being.

If I even was functional, because I sure as hell didn't feel it at the moment.

I tugged on my cock, pumping out the

last bits of my guilty spend, deciding that staying around the house wasn't as solid an idea as I had hoped it would be. So I got up, ambled to the bathroom and cleaned myself up, then decided now would probably be as good a time as ever to head out for that run, work off some of those feelings, put everything out of my mind, including the devil himself and his stupid, hot face, and then I could launch into my daily workout afterward, shower, make some dinner, and watch the latest episode of *911 Lone Star* I'd missed because I worked late last week, and call it a fucking night.

Wow, I really am boring as hell.

I changed quickly, tying on my runners, slid my keys in my shorts pocket, and took off for the walking trail. Jasper Springs Towers wasn't the biggest apartment complex in town by any means. It was nestled near the woods, which gave the place a kind of quaint, cozy atmosphere, and every day I could hear the birds out of my window tweeting away as I woke up. Mixed with the ever-present light of the sun there, it was everything I thought I could have ever wanted in a place to live. I just wished I had someone to share it with. Someone to wake up to, curled in the sheets together, while we listened to the birds sing away outside. Allie tells me it was because I'm a romantic, but I thought that sort of thing was what everyone wanted.

Wasn't it?

When I got to the trail on the side of the complex, I immediately launched into my stretches. I leaned forward, lunging to stretch my calves and legs, to limber myself up for the run. There was no one around, which made me feel a little better. Not that I minded running on the trail with other people, but there was just something about being the only one amidst the trees and plants that lined both sides of the trail. It was easier to focus, to shed whatever I needed to in my thoughts and just... be.

I stretched my arms over my head from side to side, twisting my body, pulling on my elbows as well to stretch the muscles there. I learned pretty early on, if I didn't stretch before a run, I'd be paying for it later and choking down Advil with my meals for days.

In my mindless routine, a voice cut through, breaking my concentration.

"What the hell are you doing here, Harding?"

I turned as I finished my twist, my eyes widening immediately at the sight of Dawson, dressed in nothing but silver athletic shorts and white Nikes. His tanned, muscled chest sparkled with sweat in the sunlight, his sandy hair wet. As he pulled his earbuds out, I thought I must've done some serious shit in a former life for karma to fuck me like this.

CHAPTER SEVEN

Dawson

THE LAST PERSON I ever thought I'd see on Jasper Springs Tower's trail was Nolan. For starters, I ran the track every day, rain or shine, and I'd seen a hell of a lot of people either in passing or because I'd responded to a call, or just because Jasper Springs was the smallest town on the fucking planet.

But I'd never seen Nolan anywhere outside of work until the other night at M's Place, and it seemed like ever since then I couldn't escape the infuriating adjuster who...

Looks kind of hot in that tight Under Armour tank... even with the glasses.

Especially with the glasses.
Fuck!

"Uh… I live here," he deadpanned, as if such a thing were common knowledge.

I closed my eyes immediately as I realized how dumb I must have looked, because *of course* he lived there. The property was private for residents of the Towers, which meant…

Nolan Harding lived in my damn complex and I had no freaking idea.

What were the odds?

I decided to make up for my stupid ass comment by covering up with some good old-fashioned competition, something I was far more comfortable with than talking.

Not to mention, I came to run, to feel the hard earth of the trail beneath my feet and the heat of the sun on my skin until I couldn't focus on anything else. Because that weird moment earlier, at my brother's house… left me feeling more worked up than I wanted to admit at the moment, especially to Nolan.

"Small town, small world, I guess," I grunted as I took a well-needed stop to breathe and take a drink from my water bottle.

Nolan gave me the cold shoulder, turning away from me to continue his sexy stretching, showcasing the actual definition in his arms like I was insignificant to him or his little yoga show, like he was better than me.

How dare he.

"You gonna stretch all day or you actually going to hit the pavement?" I taunted him.

Nolan turned, looking at me with dark eyes, his expression something between surprised and enticed, and I can't say it was a bad look for him.

"I would already be hitting the pavement, if you hadn't distracted me," he said with that *laissez faire* attitude of his that caused my insides to burn.

"Then by all means, Harding, don't let me get in your way," I said as I cast him a sly grin. "Race me."

I watched Nolan raise his eyebrows before sliding his hands on his hips, shaking his head. The sunlight streamed through the trees, lighting up his skin and casting shadows in all the right places.

"Dawson..."

"What? Unless you think you can't

beat me…" I said as I capped my water bottle, hooking it back on my belt.

Nolan just smirked. He fucking smirked at me!

"Oh, I'm not worried I won't beat you. I just don't want to damage your reputation," he said darkly. "Or your ego."

"Quite sure of yourself, aren't you?" I said as I took a step closer, leaving a hair's breadth between us as I looked down at his smirking face.

I expected to see his expression falter, for him to flip whatever switch it was that had turned him into that someone I got a glimpse of earlier, over the phone.

Cocky.

Self-assured.

Hot.

"Like I said, *Dawson,* you don't know what I'm capable of."

It's on, champ.

"Then let's sweeten the incentive. One race, loser buys the winner dinner."

Nolan licked his lips, shaking his head.

"You won't take no for an answer, will you?" he asked with a dark chuckle.

I shook my head, shifting my weight so I could loom over him ominously. I can't explain why, but I just felt like it would shake him. Throw him off his game, or whatever it was that was happening between us.

"I never do," I said as I started to bounce from foot to foot, readying for takeoff.

"Fine. But it's your funeral," he said as he walked away from me, taking his position at what I assumed to be our starting line, and I followed.

"Get ready to eat my dust, Harding," I said with a grin.

"Ready, set..." he called.

"Go," I snapped, taking off within seconds.

Nolan sprinted, his legs tightening as he built his rhythm, as he caught up to me, staying beside me. But I couldn't have that.

I sucked in a breath as I willed my legs to move faster, outrunning him. The breeze against my already heated skin was like a balm, and I chased that feeling; the cool air, my racing heart, and the burn in my muscles, like it was my salvation.

And maybe in a way, it was.

I smiled as we turned the bend, satisfied with my lead until Nolan caught up to me... again. His face was red and flushed, and I could see sweat starting to form on his brow, his heavy breath like an echo in the secluded space between us.

He ran a hand back through his hair, sucking in his own breath as he pushed past me.

The little fucker!

My heartbeat raced, thudding loudly in my chest as I mustered up my speed a bit, focusing intently on catching up to him.

On catching him.

Just a few more feet and we'd be homeward bound. I was beside him within seconds, focusing on my breath...

Nolan never looked at me. Instead, he kept his eyes trained on his target, our finish line.

Keeping with his pace, I knew it wouldn't be long until I hit that finish, until I claimed my prize.

Yet, I was more than surprised when Nolan pulled out a wicked sprint, taking off like a bat out of hell for the finish line, leaving me in *his* dust.

Literally, because his shoes kicked up a cloud of dirt on the trail as he all but leaped to the finish line. When he got there, he hunched over quickly, his hands on his knees as he tried to catch his breath.

He fucking beat me!

I wanted to snap, make some douchey comment, after all I'd always been a competitive man, but something about the reality of the moment left me feeling not only surprised, but proud.

Because he fucking beat me.

I huffed out a breath as I snatched my water bottle again for a drink, the only sound between us Nolan's labored breathing. He stood upright, face all flushed as he removed his shirt, using it to wipe the sweat from his face.

My gaze roved over his form, my cock stiffening at the sight of his abs.

Nolan has fucking abs?

Who would have thought?

His pale skin caught the sunlight streaming through the trees, the sweat on his very delicious, very pronounced Adonis belt that dipped into his shorts like a glowing sign.

The sudden image of me running my tongue along those groves, tasting the salt of his sweat, pushed to the forefront of my mind, and I mindlessly adjusted myself as

I watched him wipe the sweat from his forehand.

I offered him my water bottle.

"You look a little thirsty, there Nolan," I said, much darker than I'd intended.

Nolan looked back at me with fiery amber eyes, licking his pouty lips in thirst.

Fuuuuck.

Why is that so hot right now?

Nolan shuffled his weight as he shook his head. "I'm good, thanks."

"I promise I don't have cooties. Clean as a whistle in all ways that count," I said with a wink.

What the fuck?

Where did that come from?

"Seriously," I said, covering up my creepy ass comment as I took a step closer.

Nolan looked at my water bottle like it was a snake about to bite him. He took a deep breath, before grabbing it from me, his eyes never leaving mine.

"That makes two of us." He grunted as he took a long pull, and I half worried he'd drain the whole thing, but I didn't mind as I watched him guzzle my water down his throat, little streams pouring out the sides of his pretty little mouth.

Do not think sexy thoughts.

Do not think...

I hadn't had a race like that in a long time, and something about the sweat, the sunlight... a shirtless Nolan and his cocky attitude... had me feeling off my game.

"Looks like I'm buying you dinner," I said as he handed me back my water, using the back of his hand to wipe his mouth of any remaining streams of liquid.

"You don't have to..."

"A deal is a deal, Harding. And I'm a man of my word." I hooked the near empty bottle back onto my belt.

"Not going to take no for an answer, I take it?"

"Got somewhere you want to go tonight?" I asked nonchalantly.

"Tonight?" Nolan asked, his eyes widening in surprise. "Oh, I didn't—"

"You got plans I don't know about?" I taunted him.

Nolan shrugged.

"I mean, I was going to catch up on the latest episode of *911 Lone Star*," he said, clearing his throat. "But, uh..."

"Ouch. You really know how to dig the blade in, don't you?" I said, shaking my head.

"I didn't mean..."

"I'll pick you up tomorrow at six. Be ready," I said.

"But I—"

I smirked at him as I made my way off the trail, and just as I expected, he followed me like a good little lamb.

"Wouldn't want to get in the way of your TK and Carlos marathon," I said with a wink, which caused a blush to spread across Nolan's nose and into his cheeks.

He does that a lot, it's kind of... cute.

Though he couldn't see the grin on my face, I couldn't help myself.

Sometimes he just made things so easy.

CHAPTER EIGHT

Nolan

THE REALITY OF the situation hit me, making my already racing heart beat faster.

I beat Dawson, which meant...
Fuck.
He's buying me dinner.
Tomorrow night.

A part of me was more than ecstatic to spend an evening with *Mr. March* himself, because in some weird, twisted way, I thought this would be the only way I *could* spend time with my two year long fireman crush.

It was just happenstance that we both lived at the Towers, some sense of serendipity or a cruel twist of fate that we'd both ended up on the same trail at the same time.

By the time I caught up to Dawson, I'd started to cool down from our run, but my heart still raced. Dawson nonchalantly held the door for me after he'd gone inside the main lobby entrance. He cast me a smirk over his tanned shoulder that warmed my insides like molten lava.

"Thanks," I said, focusing on sounding like a normal, even-toned human, even though my breath was threatening to catch in my throat again.

"Don't mention it," he said with a snicker as he headed for the elevator.

Shit, that means he's not on this floor.

I casually strolled up beside him as he pressed the up button, feeling strangely on the spot.

Say something, or it's going to get awkward.

"I got out of work early today," I said, like a weirdo, feeling an ever-present need to explain myself.

Dawson shrugged. "Surprised you aren't holed up in your apartment working. Do you even know how to relax?"

"Of course, I know how to relax..." I

huffed, fully rising to his bait, noting the way the corner's of Dawson's lips turned up when I did.

He's fucking playing with me. Is he...

Is he flirting *with me?*

"Running off all that pent up frustration isn't relaxing, you know."

"Watching tv is relaxing."

"No, it's not. It's mindless. It's something to focus on because you need to fill your space."

I crossed my arms as I watched the floors light up. Three more floors.

"And just how do you relax, Dawson?"

He smiled sexily, his tongue darting out to lick his lips before he spoke, and damn if it didn't make my cock twitch.

I wonder just how many licks it'd take him to get the center of my fucking tootsie roll pop...

"I don't give up all my secrets before a first date, Nolan. You'll just have to wait and see," he said as the elevator dinged, opening for us both ominously. Dawson looked back to me with a grin as he waved forward.

"After you, champ," he taunted me. I stepped in without looking back, but the heat radiating off of Dawson could be felt like it was its own entity. I leaned over to press the second floor, feeling somewhat sheepish that I could have forgone this awkward scenario and taken the stairs, but sue me... I wanted to keep Dawson to myself just a little while longer. At least until we'd split to our humble abodes, where he could rethink everything.

When he was in, the doors closed instantly, and I watched as he pressed his floor. He was on the third floor.

My heart thudded away in my chest so loud I thought it would echo in the enclosed space, thought perhaps Dawson could hear it just from standing next to me. I kept my gaze trained on the lights.

Dawson nudged me. "I haven't had anyone give me a run for my money like that in a while. We should do this again sometime," he said the words genuinely, causing me to turn in surprise. Only then did I notice he'd somehow gotten closer. He leaned his arm out against the wall, leaning languidly as his amber eyes met mine. Everything about him exuded sex appeal—his shirtless, well-defined form, his semi-wet sandy blond hair, his dark, enticing eyes. His perfect lips that begged to be kissed.

To be ravished and owned.

I let out a shaky breath as my gaze fell to those lips, licking my own as I fought the desire to close the space between us, to put this elevator on hold and do what I'd been dreaming about for two years.

But because I'm a cursed man, that was the exact moment the elevator dinged, opening to my floor.

"I think that's your floor, champ," he said, his gaze full of heat as it dipped to my lips, his voice suddenly quite gravelly.

"Right, my floor... 911... marathon."

"Have a good night, Nolan. I'll see you tomorrow night," he said definitively, and it took all my concentration to move my sore legs, to walk out of that elevator with my dignity.

The doors started to close, and I realized I hadn't asked where we were going.

A part of me thought maybe it was a fruitless endeavor, after all, he could change his mind by tomorrow, but maybe I just wanted one more moment, one last glance at the man of my dreams before it all went up in flames.

I stopped the doors with a palm, and Dawson shifted his stance, his gaze still full of fire.

"Where are we going? Tomorrow? I need to know so I know how to—"

"Now, now, where would the fun be in telling you? I'd rather make you sweat. Hot and bothered is a good look on you," he drawled as he gently pushed my arm away, and the doors slowly slid closed.

My mouth gaped as I watched the doors close, taking Dawson up to third floor, leaving me stiff, hot, and full of panic.

I can't fuck this up.

This might be closest I ever get to a date with Dawson Richards.

Because it wasn't a date by any means. Dawson was a man of his word, and I'd won fair and square. It was just good sportsmanship, nothing more.

Even if I wanted it to be...

So, as I gathered myself and headed down the hall to my apartment, I promised myself I would do whatever it took to make the one shot I had absolutely perfect.

CHAPTER NINE

Dawson

I'D NEVER BEEN so relieved to be cut off by an elevator in my life.

I just couldn't seem to help myself around Nolan. I *liked* pushing his buttons, throwing him off guard and causing a little chaos to his daily routine, I could admit that at least.

But there was a moment, in that elevator where I'd forgotten who we were, where we were.

As I leaned against the wall, staring down at those pouty, perfect lips, I thought *fuck, this is it. This is my sexual harassment suit in the making.*

I sighed as the doors opened on my

floor, thanking the heavens above for the brief moment of reality.

My body was flushed, still hot, and I was certain it wasn't entirely from the run.

Once in my apartment, I could relax. Or at least, that's what I intended on doing. Shower, clean up a bit, maybe get some take out before I headed back to the firehouse. I stared at my phone on the counter, feeling a little antsy.

It'd been a weird fucking day, and a part of me wanted to call my best friend and dish about all the grade A tea. About that hot-as-hell phone call, Nolan showing up at my brother's... that hot-as-hell race, and me nearly losing all my fucking marbles in that damn elevator.

But a part of me also knew that Cade was in that new relationship haze.

Which meant for him nothing would matter except the man he was all twitterpated for at the moment; a man who was actually *good* for him. I wanted things to really work out for them.

I wasn't lying when I said what I did at M's Place the other night. I wanted to see my ex turned bestie settle down and have the life he always wanted. I sighed, shaking my head.

What about what *I wanted?*

Did I want some white picket fence, brunch on Sundays sort of life that everyone around here seemed accustomed to?

I swear, sometimes it's like the Stepford Wives up in here.

I'd always known what I *didn't* want. But knowing what I did want... I wasn't so sure what that was.

There was a sort of rhythm to being a bachelor. To living life the way I had, without attachments. I'd had boyfriends, sure, but I hadn't been on a *date* somewhere like Sedona in a while. I knew immediately I'd wanted to take Nolan there, not only because I knew it would shock him—I doubted the pencil pusher had been anywhere like the five-star restaurant in the city that's famous for its cocktails and it's flaming tower dessert— but because for some reason I couldn't explain... I wanted to *impress* him.

I wanted the chance to show this pain in the ass that I wasn't just some dumb, charismatic asshole who lived to make his life hell.

Even though I do enjoy raining hell

down on him.

Why do I care what Nolan Harding thinks of me?

I slid out of my shorts, groaning in defeat as I headed for the bathroom, the cool air of my apartment kissing my skin.

I knew the answer, even if I didn't want to admit it.

Because maybe this was fate giving us a second chance.

A do-over.

Not that he remembers anyway, that's clear.

I turned the water on in the shower as I let my thoughts wander to two years ago, the day I met Nolan.

I'd just gotten out of a relationship with my ex, Vance, who worked for the same company Nolan did, Breisinger Insurance.

It had been a rocky relationship from the start, and I knew he wasn't going to stick around—after all, he was planning to move if he got his dream job at some accounting firm he'd been hard on since college. Breisinger Insurance was just a pit stop for him. Something to pay the bills until he could squirrel his pennies and get the fuck out of Jasper Springs. I knew that, and it wasn't like I was after anything serious either. Or at least, that was what I told myself.

But somewhere in my feeble, stupid, romantic brain I thought maybe, just maybe *I'd be enough.*

I wanted to be enough.

But I wasn't.

He broke it off with me and no sooner was he packed and out the door, blowing dust in my direction. I wasn't in love with the guy or anything, but it still stung. I'd become used to having another person in my bed, in my space, and suddenly... it was cold.

Lonely.

Breisinger didn't wait until the ink even dried on Vance's two weeks notice before they brought in Nolan.

A dark-haired young buck who looked like some cross between Hot Harry Potter from a B-produced porno and your little sister's math tutor.

Vance left, and there wasn't even a mourning period. He'd been replaced, and it made me feel like I'd been replaced too.

I wanted to hate Nolan Harding. And I did, for a while. I hated his doe-eyed face, his nitpicking, his refusal to talk or gossip with anyone, especially me.

His little snide comments he thought I didn't hear in passing when we'd see each other on the job.

But I was starting to realize that perhaps there was more to Nolan than I'd thought, and maybe I didn't *actually* hate the guy.

Maybe I was actually starting to... like him.

I jumped in the shower immediately upon that thought, needing the cold water to wash away my thoughts and feelings.

One thing at a time.

CHAPTER TEN

Dawson

AFTER A LONG day of calls, I was practically butter in the shower. I wasn't sure why I was so nervous.

It wasn't like I'd never been on a date, and I certainly knew how to show a guy a good time. Yet, I found myself distracted now that I was done for the day and the hours were dwindling closer until I'd have to pick up Nolan and whisk him away to reap the reward of his winnings.

Hey...

I almost couldn't believe the text that had come through from Nolan—who I affectionately had listed in my phone as Fucking Asshole—and I did a double take.

Nolan never texted me. If he needed to reach me about anything, he usually called, albeit most of those calls where always when I was in the middle of something, so this was new.

Heyyyyy, I texted back if only to be an asshole myself and be sarcastic. *Where's the fire?* I asked cheekily.

There is no fire.

I rolled my eyes, clearly Fucking Asshole's sense of humor was hit or miss.

I know that, asshole. You just never text me, so I assumed something was of dire importance.

I watched as those three little bubbles appeared on the screen, imagining Nolan tapping away furiously.

Right, of course, I just wanted to let you know I followed up on your brother's claim.

I leaned against the fire truck as I read his message.

You couldn't just call to tell me that? I asked.

I'm not in the office today. Verizon is still working on the lines.

A part of me knew I should keep things professional. After all, we worked together and I didn't want things to get weird, especially since as far as work was concerned. Nolan was helping me out and we were somewhat getting along. The last thing I needed was to piss him off when he was the one overseeing my brother's claim.

But hell if I wasn't a glutton for punishment and bad decisions, and maybe I needed something to take the edge off of my uncharacteristic nerves regarding our date tonight.

It's not a date.

Not really...

I'd told myself that over and over since the day prior, when I'd told Nolan I was a man of my word. It wasn't a date.

But it didn't feel like a business meeting either.

Instead of falling down that rabbit hole, I decided to push thoughts of our date–not date out of my mind.

And antagonize Nerdy Nolan a bit, if only because I considered it one of my favorite hobbies.

So what you're telling me is you're home... alone. Working.

I watched the text bubbles dance in wait of his reply.

I am, I thought we established this... he texted. I could hear the exasperation in his tiny little digital letters on the screen as text bubbles popped up again.

I just wanted to let you know everything was processed. I'll keep an eye on this claim, and let you know if anything comes up.

Suddenly, I felt like an ass. I let out a sigh as I realized he was probably just trying to help, and I'd been an asshole taking advantage of the situation to what?

Flirt?

Make him all flustered?

Like some insensitive idiot.

Thanks, I appreciate it. Really.

It seemed forever until he'd texted me back.

Work's been a little crazy as of late, but you made it pretty clear this is important to you, so it's important to me too.

I wasn't sure how to respond to that. I knew Nolan was being professional, despite my attempts to make things unprofessional by flirting, but a part of me also wanted to hope that maybe there was more to his words.

I wasn't the kind of guy to ask for help with anything. I was the guy who always swooped in and rescued other people. But the idea that someone would back me up, support the things that were important to me because it's who they were or what was right, was something I was lacking in my life.

Before I could respond, those little bubbles started to come up again.

I knew I should just let it go, thank him, and be done with shit. But the weird hope that had somehow blossomed in my chest and my ever-present need to take something serious and make it less serious won out.

You know what else is important to me, Nolan?

The bubbles disappeared.

After a moment of no response, I thought perhaps he'd ended the conversation, or that he'd gone off to do something else, leaving me hanging on the edge.

Rude.

But soon enough a *?* came through.

A strange sense of relief flooded me.

He's still there... I thought.

Your apartment number.

Truth be told, I kind of already knew since he was one floor below me, and I had access to such knowledge because I'd been on enough cases at the Towers that finding his apartment wasn't all that difficult, but it felt sort of like an overreach if I just showed up at his door unannounced. While I saw something like that as romantic and fun, someone shy and quiet like Nolan might feel like their privacy was violated.

Boundaries and all.

So I figured now would be as good as a time as ever to ask.

Why do you need to know my apartment number? I can just meet you wherever...

A part of me wondered if Nolan regretted agreeing to this dinner. He seemed a bit skittish, or nervous even.

But I wasn't letting him off the hook. If all I had was this one chance to put this all to rest, put Nolan out of my mind entirely, I needed to see this through.

Besides who doesn't want to go to a fancy restaurant with a hot guy and enjoy themselves for a night?

I typed out my reply quickly. *Well, if you lived in a house, I'd ride up in my trusty steed and pick you up from your doorstep like a true gentlemen.*

Nolan quickly responded. *Somehow, I have a hard time believing you are a gentleman in any facet of life.*

My smile spread as excitement took hold.

That little fucker!

I tapped out the words in rapid pace. *I can be whoever you want me to be, baby. As long as you're dressed in something nice and ready for me to pick you up at your door at six o'clock. No takebacks.*

I hit send, then immediately sent another text after I realized how desperate I sounded.

Was I really this desperate?

Yes, yes I was.

Desperate for something different, for a chance to forget about my boring life, about my brother's claim, which apparently was 'being handled' by Nolan now, about the fact that I hadn't had a successful relationship with someone other than my hand in at least two years.

Unless all you have is twelve pairs of white shirts and khakis, which then I might have to call 911 and report a fashion emergency.

A smirk played at my lips, a chuckle forming in my throat.

Nolan took my bait. Hook, line, and sinker.

I loved how easy it was to ruffle his feathers. It was entertaining as hell.

I will have you know, I own far more than just white shirts and khakis! I can look nice *if I want to. I can look even nicer if you tell me where we are going.*

I shook my head, typing back, *Not a chance, champ. Just be ready for me. Six o'clock. I'll pick you up and we'll head there in my truck. No sense in us taking two cars anyway, since we are both going back to the same place.*

That was the moment Gina called me from across the room, nipping at me to get off my phone and get my ass in the house to help Frank, our newest rookie with something.

Gotta go. I'll see you tonight.

CHAPTER ELEVEN

Nolan

"THERE'S NO NEED to panic," Allie said calmly as I paced across my bedroom.

Her disembodied voice was not helping matters as she watched me from FaceTime like I was some anxious animal.

Because I am an anxious animal.

"Of course, there is a need to panic! I haven't been on a date in like five years, Allie. I need... I need this to go well, you know. Not just because it's Dawson, but..."

Because I need to know I'm not a complete failure of a human being.

"I thought you said it *wasn't* a date. That it was just a silly bet. That it's just you besting him and getting your reward."

I huffed out a groan of defeat. "I know what I said, but..."

Truth was, up until I'd texted Dawson, I was content to believe it was just some silly bet, nothing to get worked up over. I'd put on some nice clothes, smile, and enjoy wherever we were going solely because it was a night out with the man I've been pining over for the last two years, and quite frankly, I was starting to think Karla was right. Maybe I *did* need a break, maybe I did need to relax.

But after Dawson's weirdly flirtatious texts earlier about making sure I looked nice, how he'd called me *baby*... telling me to be ready when *he* picked me up.

Well, it kind of sounded like maybe this *was* a date, which I knew was crazy. After all, Dawson Richards could have any man he wanted. He'd only have to blink and they'd say, "Yes, Daddy, take me home and ruin me."

Myself included.

I'd won the race fair and square, but as I second-guessed everything in my closet earlier, I felt more like a loser than a winner in anything.

I'm so out of my league here.

"Then why do I feel like a high-schooler going out with the captain of the football team?" I grumbled as I smoothed the front of my light blue button down for the hundredth time in an hour.

Staring at myself in the mirror, I had to admit I did look *nice.* My shirtsleeves were rolled up to the elbows, which I felt showed off my arms nicely, especially since I'd been working out a lot more since the beginning of the year. I wasn't built like Dawson or the other firefighters, but I liked where my definition was going, and I knew if I kept it up, it would only get better.

I stared at my mirror image, my pale skin contrasting the perfectly crisp pale blue shirt and a nice tailored pair of slacks, my dark hair swept back just enough to look like I hadn't spent a half hour strategically arranging it in front of my bathroom mirror. Even my glasses looked nice with the outfit. It was a simple look, but I'd found through the years that sometimes simple was best. It's often understated, but I'd gotten through plenty of weddings, cocktail parties, and business meetings with that outfit.

As I looked at myself, I felt a pang in

my heart. I wanted to look more than *nice.* I wanted to look like someone who could be on a date with *Mr. March.*

I wanted to look *sexy.*

I wanted to *feel* sexy.

Sigh.

That was when I heard the knock on my door, which made me nearly jump out of my clothes and skin as my gaze flashed to my digital clock. It was only five fifty-three.

He's a couple minutes early.

I ran to grab my phone from its stand, Allie's eyes lighting up with excitement.

"Holy shit, he's here..." I gulped, watching Allie smile ear to ear.

"You're going to have a great time, Nolan. I promise. Just be yourself."

I wished I could be anyone else, truly.

Someone whose heart wasn't ready to beat out of his chest with anxiety right about now.

"Right, I'll call you later," I said as I ended our call.

Dawson rapped on my door again, causing an involuntary reaction of annoyance.

"I'm coming, hold your horses," I bit out as I power-walked through my apartment to the door. When I got there, I took a deep breath.

It's now or never, Nolan.

I opened the door and I immediately thought I must have died.

Had a heart attack five minutes ago when the reality that I was going on a date with Dawson set in.

Because the sight of the man in front of me was damn near breath-stealing.

Dawson leaned against my doorframe, the position showcasing his sexy-as-fuck arm muscles. He was also dressed in a button down, but from the sight of it, it looked like silk, and it was a deep ochre. The color against his naturally tanned skin made him look golden, like some sun god. His brownish-blonde hair fell in his eyes a bit, in a rogue, unkempt sort of way that somehow looked both refined and chaotically beautiful. My gaze roved over his form from head to toe, noting that the slacks he was wearing were perfectly tight around his hips where his gold belt caught the light from above, glittering like a glowing sign that pointed directly to his...

"Wow," was all I could say, like a fucking idiot.

Yup, totally out of my league here.

Dawson's pretty lips curved into a wicked smile as he raised an eyebrow.

"Like what you see, Harding?" he teased.

I nodded, swallowing nervously.

"You look... nice."

Dawson smirked. "Just nice?" His voice was dark and inviting, and I had half a mind to pull him into my fucking apartment and kiss him until I couldn't breathe.

But I needed to remain cool, collected. I couldn't afford to fuck this up. I wanted this night to be perfect.

Grabbing Dawson and sequestering him in my apartment like a creepy stalker is not perfect by any means.

I shrugged, collecting my surprise and putting on my best impression of a normal person.

"I mean, I prefer you in your uniform, but that's just me."

Why the fuck did I say that?

I'm supposed to be acting normal!

Dawson didn't miss a beat though, taking my moment of lunacy and running with it.

"Didn't peg you for a badge bunny,

champ."

"I'm not," I huffed in defense. "You're early..." I said, avoiding his gaze, if only so he couldn't see my blush.

Truth was, I'd never been into service men of any kind, despite the fact I'd been working with them for a while.

I didn't really have a type, to be honest. The only men I'd ever had relationships with tended to be like me. Quiet, reserved, and most certainly not the type to run into a burning building or pose in their underwear for calendars.

"Don't do that," he admonished darkly as he gently tugged my chin to face him, making my entire body flush with heat.

The flush in my face had to be insanely prevalent and as close to a steamed tomato as humanly possible, judging from the heat that had overtaken me.

"Do what?" I breathed, my voice much huskier than I intended it to be, my gaze downcast.

"Look at me when you talk to me."

My insides twisted as I realized he hadn't let go of me. Trapped in his fiery gaze, I felt myself crumbling like a stack of cards. My gaze flashed up to meet his.

"I'm sorry, I..."

"Don't apologize, Nolan. You clean up nice too, you know," he said softly, his thumb brushing the underside of my chin as he gazed back at me, his tongue darting out to lick his lips.

Which caused my cock to wake the fuck up.

I felt my blush spread across my cheeks, my instinct to turn away, but Dawson's fingers held me in place.

"Are you nervous, Nolan?" His voice was playful, but enticing all the same. Like yesterday when we'd talked on the phone.

The memory of that moment only made my cock twitch.

Like an idiot I said, "I'm just... hungry, I guess."

I *was* hungry. But I wasn't sure if it was for food or for... him.

Maybe a little of both.

A wicked smile graced his lips as he let go of my chin, and I hated that my skin felt colder without his touch.

"Me too, champ. Let's go," he said as he turned away, leading me down the hall to the elevator, my head spinning and my cock aching.

What the fuck have I gotten myself into?

CHAPTER TWELVE

Nolan

I SAT IN Dawson's candy apple red truck, feeling like I was going to pass out. I set my hands on my thighs, if only so my pants would absorb the sweat from my palms.

Dawson crawled into the driver's seat, and cranking the ignition. Music blared from the speakers, some Nickelback song that I didn't know all the lyrics to.

"Are you going to tell me where we're going yet? Or are you going to blindfold me?" I drawled sarcastically.

Dawson flashed me a smirk. "That depends, do you want me to blindfold you?"

The darkness in his voice called to my cock like a damn siren and I shifted in my seat, trying my hardest to quell my burgeoning erection as I looked out the window so he couldn't see my blush.

"No, thank you," I said with a cough and a swallow.

No way in hell was I walking into that trap. The last thing I needed was to come in my pants sitting next to the man of my dreams before we even got to the fucking restaurant.

Christ, I haven't felt this horny since I discovered I liked cock.

Dawson chuckled as he pulled the car out of the Towers parking lot.

And he didn't say a word. He only focused on the road, his lips pursed. Gone was the playfulness, the sexy banter, and in its place was an awkward tension that filled the space.

I looked over at him, wondering if I'd said something wrong, done something, or if maybe he was just regretting this whole situation altogether. Whatever it was, I decided to try and break the ice.

The speakers blared with *Theory Of A Deadman*, which I knew only because in high school the guy I dated was obsessed with the band. A part of me felt inclined to scoot closer, to close the space between us, but I didn't.

"Can you at least tell me if where we're going is close?" I asked.

Dawson turned briefly to look at me.

"About a half hour. Why, you got some other pressing engagement tonight? Another tv marathon?" he said, but his voice was not playful or fun. Instead, it was replaced with a bit of anger.

My eyebrows furrowed and I shook my head.

"Nope. I'm all yours this evening." I swallowed as I said the words, but they weren't as difficult to speak as I thought they would be.

Dawson's shoulders loosened a fraction as he pursed his lips.

Some band I didn't recognize came over the speakers, the singer practically screaming and making my ears ring as they sang about the sound of madness.

"How can you listen to this stuff? It's just freaking noise," I said.

Dawson huffed out a sigh of annoyance.

"*Shinedown* is not noise," Dawson said defensively.

"Well, not to you. But it's a little grating on my ears," I half-whined, following it with a pout.

Dawson shot me a look that I could only describe as domineering, and I half worried he was going to pull this car over and murder me for my disdain of what was clearly his favorite music.

Way to go, Nolan.

"You know," I started as I sat back in my seat, crossing my arms. "Technically, the winner should pick the music," I quipped.

That seemed to alter his mood a bit, replacing the moody Dawson in front of me with the charismatic Dawson I was used to.

"Bratty boys don't always get what they want. Sometimes they have to work for it," he teased back, flashing a half-smile.

I couldn't help that my mouth dropped open at his words.

Was he calling me a... brat?

The notion made me turn six shades of red, and Dawson only shook his head, a complete smile finally spreading across his face.

"Fucking hell, Nolan, you need to stop

doing that," he said, chuckling.

"Doing what?"

"Being fucking cute," he said, flashing me a grin as he hit his steering wheel.

Dawson thinks I'm... cute?

The words caused me to choke on my own air.

No fucking way.

He shook his head. "Driver picks the music, champ. Maybe if you're a good boy though... you can pick it on the way home." His voice was dark and enticing and my cock throbbed from the implications.

I shifted in my seat once more, casually adjusting myself in a way that wouldn't draw attention.

The last thing I needed was for Dawson to know just how freaking turned on I was at the moment.

Because I most definitely found Dawson Richards more than *cute*.

He was freaking perfect.

Too perfect for someone like me, and I was dancing dangerously close to the edge of Heaven. So, I decided if I was going to die on this hill, I was going to go down in style.

"Oh, I can be *very good*," I said,

flashing him with a grin of my own. "With proper incentive, that is. I like rewards."

"Of course you do," he said as he continued to drive, turning up the radio.

But I didn't fight him on it. Instead, I just let myself take in the sight of him dressed like a fucking snack, the wind messing up his hair through the window, and I committed the perfect image to my memory.

Because I knew after all was said and done, that's all I'd have.

CHAPTER THIRTEEN

Dawson

I PARKED THE car, my mind racing and my pulse thudding away like a steel drum. I turned to look at Nolan, to take in the sight of his face, but instead I found him staring at *me.*

"You didn't have to do this," he said, his cheeks still holding his color from the heat of the outdoors mixed with his natural demeanor.

I wasn't lying when I'd told him he needed to quit with the bashful antics. I swear, every time the man sported a blush it made my cock rise to attention, made my heart skip a beat.

Not to mention it made me think about

other things... like wondering if his pale ass would brighten like his face if I took my hand to it.

Fuck, now is not the time for sexy thoughts!

I internally chastised myself as I cleared my throat.

"I told you I'm a man of my word," I said as I leaned back against my seat.

Nolan sighed. "I know, but this... this is expensive and fancy, and..."

"And what? I can't like expensive, fancy things?"

"That's not what I'm saying. It's just... I would have been fine with..."

I watched as his eyebrows furrowed, as his shoulders tightened as he looked from me to the sleek building in front of us.

"Not many people in Jasper Springs can undermine me quite like you, Nolan. You beat me, and that's not something I take lightly. Great things deserve great rewards." I shrugged as I opened my door, hurrying to his before he could open it himself. I pulled the door open to see glassy brown eyes staring at me over his glasses, and I stepped to the side, if only to give him room to get out, but also because...

Because if I stood any closer, we might not have made it into the damn restaurant.

"I do not *undermine* you," he grumbled as he crossed his arms.

I closed the door, casting him a smirk. "I know this is a difficult concept to grasp for you, but maybe I think you're worth it, champ. It's not everyday someone hands my ass to me on a silver platter."

Nolan softened a tad. "That's because not everyone can keep up with your fine ass in order to do so."

I smiled both at his words and at the way they made him blush.

Sweet Jesus, grant me the strength to make it through this dinner without busting a damn nut.

"Shall we?" I said as I slid my hands in my pockets.

Nolan sighed, nodding in approval. "Lead the way."

CHAPTER FOURTEEN

Dawson

"I'M SORRY MR. RICHARDS, but your table isn't quite ready yet," the hostess said in the most graceful tone possible. I knew we were early, but I guess I had not realized *how* early. I really put the pedal to the medal, arriving a whole *twenty minutes early*. To be fair, there was no traffic, and I guess all that nervous energy got channeled into my lead foot.

"It's fine," "Nolan said, kindly and politely as I sighed. This date was off to a terrible start. Not only had I managed to sound like an absolute ass in the car, but now we were going to have to wait around for twenty or so minutes until we could eat, and I was seriously starving.

"You can find us at the bar, when it's ready," I said with a shrug, flashing her a smile and turning to make my way to the onyx bar.

Sedona itself was pretty uppity in its design but the bar was something else entirely. Long, sleek, shimmering black onyx from one end to the other, the gemstone and resin design was one that could only be appreciated up close. The top of the bar itself looked like one of those cracked geode rocks from fourth grade science class but much sexier, and the bottles of top-shelf liquor were lit from behind with blues and purples that made even the bottles themselves look divine.

"What can I get you, sir?" the bartender asked, his vague transatlantic accent perfectly in line with the aesthetic of the place.

"What you got on tap?" I asked, noting Nolan approached the bar slowly, picking up an acrylic table sign of drink specials, looking nonplussed.

The bartender slowly rambled on, but I couldn't focus on his words. All I could focus on was Nolan. His skin lit up with the outlying glow of the lights behind the bar, biting his perfect pout. Which made me swallow hard, made my cock twitch.

"Sir?" the man asked me again, and I realized I must have completely tuned him out, so I waved my hand, nodding with a smile. "The last one," I said, hoping to hell that whatever it was I just ordered wouldn't be dry and bitter as hell.

"And for you, sir?" the bartender turned to Nolan, his lips pulling up in the corner. It was the smallest smile, but it was a smile I hadn't been given.

Oh no, you don't, asshole. This one's mine.

Immediately, I froze upon my thoughts as Nolan looked up from his drink specials, big brown eyes oblivious to the bartender's subtle flirt.

I'd never thought of Nolan as much more than a thorn in my side for the last two years—well, unless you counted my fantasies but that was different.

Because fantasy was certainly not reality, and the reality was that Nolan didn't belong to me, not even in the slightest. He drove me damn near to drink with his incessant nitpicking and oversight of the claims I filed, and aggravated the hell out of me with his uncanny way of showing up just when I didn't want him to, but it seemed like somewhere along the line, my entire brain had done a complete one eighty.

The reality was that at some point, whether it was the race, or him showing up to *take care* of my brother because it was important to me, or maybe it was the night he showed up at M's Place and won bingo... somewhere along the line I'd changed, and I no longer wanted to make Nolan's life a living hell.

I just wanted *him.*

To make his cheeks turn scarlet, to get him so flustered he couldn't speak, to fuck him so good he wouldn't be able to leave his fucking couch.

I swallowed harshly as that reality set in, because I knew this wasn't a date.

But maybe I wanted it to be.

So, I decided if this date-not-date was going to be a disaster, I might as well make it a pretty one.

"Oh, uh, I'm not..."

"Tell the nice man what you want, baby," I taunted him, which made him flush.

Dawson 1, Nolan 10, bartender 0.

"If you have questions or would like a

recommendation," the bartender said smoothly as he leaned his arms across the surface, his voice smooth and rich like the bar itself.

Nolan set the drink specials down, chewing on his lip as if contemplating what to order with great thought.

"I'll have the Elderberry Fizz. Please," he said poignantly.

"Will that be all, sir?" the bartender asked, his voice huskier than I liked.

I moved closer to Nolan, only by an inch, placing my hand at the small of his back, which made Nolan jump nearly five feet off the ground.

"See, now was that so hard?" I teased.

Nolan side-eyed me from underneath his thick, black glasses and smirked. "You are insufferable, you know that?" he said as he cocked his head to the side, blowing a stray piece of hair out of his eyes.

"It is my number one goal in life. To be an insufferable bastard," I said, flashing him with a grin as I turned to look at the bartender. "That'll be all, thanks."

Twenty minutes turned into thirty minutes, as there had been a party before us who was in our spot, who just didn't seem to want to leave. Normally, I would have argued, gotten angry that I was planning on spending good money there too, so why the hell wasn't I capable of being seated on time, but I'd already accepted this date-not-date was an epic disaster, so what else could I do? Especially after two beers of my own, knowing I needed to slow down or we'd be catching an Uber home.

Which didn't sound bad, but then again, I didn't want an audience with Nolan. In fact, I didn't want *anyone* else with Nolan but me.

Mine.

All mine.

My buzzed thoughts wandered to places they shouldn't, my little Nolan fantasies threatening to take the driver's seat.

Despite his cocky, bratty attitude at times, Nolan hadn't been the clearest on his signals. While I knew without a doubt at this point he did in fact like guys, and he'd made a few comments about me and my calendar shoots, I wasn't entirely sure if he liked... me.

He did insult your taste in music.

Whether or not he liked me—the me

underneath the charisma and the humor—shouldn't have mattered to me at all.

Why did I care if he liked me?

It wasn't like every man I fucked in my life liked me for my winning personality. Sex was just that, sex.

And sometimes it was way hotter when I was balls deep in some pretty asshole that didn't respect me or like me *at all.*

But my feeble, inebriated mind warred with my heart and my hunger, desiring something more.

I wanted him to like me, because I liked him. More than I ever thought I would.

We followed the waiter, who was dressed in a get up that looked strangely reminiscent of a penguin, Nolan giggling the entire way. After the second Elderberry Fizz, he seemed to have loosened up and I wasn't complaining.

Once we'd both ordered our meals, and the waiter had left us once again, I had Nolan all to myself, which I enjoyed far too much.

"Glad to see you're enjoying yourself," I said genuinely, relishing in the smile that formed across his face. He nodded.

God he has a nice smile.

My entire body loosened at the sight.

Shit, I definitely need to stick with water.

"I am, actually. I... I can't remember the last time I've even done something like this."

"Like what?" I asked involuntarily, and took a sip of my water.

"I mean, it's been awhile since I've been out on a date in general, let alone with someone like you," Nolan said as he spun his stir stick in his drink.

"What do you mean, like me?" I asked, confused.

"Confident, brave. Sexy," he said, and he took another drink, hiding his blush behind his glass. But I wasn't about to let him off the hook. Not now when he seemed keen on dishing out compliments.

I'm a sucker for a little praise, so sue me.

But something about the way he said the words felt deeply genuine, and I couldn't help but rise to his bait, especially because it made me feel like I'd just won bar bingo.

Well, well... maybe I should take Nolan out for a drink more often.

"Is that so?" I said as I tapped my fingers on the table, steeling my gaze on his pink cheeks. "You think I'm... sexy? Is that why you're always up my ass?" I teased him, my own smile forcing its way across my face.

Nolan shook his head. "I mean, how many times have you gotten naked for the damn calendar? Like four times?"

"You counted?" I asked coyly.

Nolan shrugged, taking another sip of his drink. "Absolutely not,"

Liar.

"You know, you're not quite what I thought you were either. For the record." The words came out of my mouth of their own volition, causing Nolan to peer up at me over his thick frames.

"Wha... what do you mean?" he stuttered.

"I mean, don't get me wrong, you're still a giant pain in my ass, but I thought... I thought I knew you. But I'm just starting to scratch the surface, I think."

Nolan looked up at me with big, bright puppy dog eyes, his entire expression shifting like I'd just told him the last piece of cake was his.

As far as I'm concerned, he can have whatever he wants tonight... and I do hope there's cake.

"I hope that's not a bad thing," he whispered, his eyebrows furrowing.

Oh you sweet, sweet man...

Who the hell burned you?

I looked him in the eye, mustering as much seriousness as I could when I said, "No, Nolan. Not at all. In fact, I—"

Before I could spill all my secrets and newfound desires out on the table like a teenage girl, the waiter came with our food, shattering the strange sort of tension that had grown between us, and neither of us had any thoughts about anything but the absolutely fantastic food in front of us.

When we'd both devoured our meals plus dessert—a delectable chocolate horchata cake—and the check came, Nolan immediately tried to grab it.

"Ah, ah... paws off, baby."

"Come on, we can split it. You don't have to—"

"I want to, Nolan. Seriously, just let..." I sighed as I watched his face intently.

"Just let me take care of *you.*"

CHAPTER FIFTEEN

Nolan

THE ELDERBERRY FIZZES must have gone to my head. There was no other way I could explain the complete disconnect that happened in my brain and body when Dawson told me he wanted to *take care of me.*

It was like an out of body experience. I'd had two serious boyfriends in my short, twenty-eight years of life. Well, one wasn't really my boyfriend, he was more or less trying to figure his shit out, but we weren't in the closet or anything, so I think it counts.

Because if it didn't, that would mean I've only ever been in one serious relationship my entire life.

Sure, I'd thought of scenarios like this one when I was alone—usually because the crux of my thoughts were centered around what would happen *after* I'd been sufficiently wined and dined by a handsome man with eyes only for me, and usually in those thoughts, I ended up on my knees showing my praise and putting out like a homecoming queen.

God, I am so easy!

But I never thought I'd actually be here, in this situation, with Dawson Richards of all people.

Despite the alcohol, I found myself unable to speak, even though my thoughts were running a mile a minute.

Dawson's eyebrows furrowed and he narrowed his gaze at me as he handed the check and his credit card to the waiter.

"I—" I cleared my throat, finding the will to speak once more if only because I didn't want to seem rude.

"Thank... you," I managed to get the words out.

Dawson cast a smile I could only describe as dirty and wicked at me, his brown eyes lighting up with the signature golden energy that encapsulated him most of the time.

Drawing me closer, like a bug to the sun.

"Don't thank me just yet. Wait till we get home," he said, flashing me a flirtatious wink, causing my blush to hit me like a tidal wave.

I both hated and loved that with barely a few words and a look, this man could have me so flushed and flustered, so damn desperate for more of that hot, golden light that only he could shine.

I wanted more.

Stupidly, I wanted anything Dawson was willing to give me.

I sucked down the remainder of my third fizzy drink, feeling much more relaxed than I usually did. I wasn't sure what all the bartender put in that thing, but whatever it was, it was making me feel on cloud nine, invincible almost.

Which probably accounted for my sudden influx of confidence at the moment.

Because as I watched Dawson sign his receipt and slide his credit card back into his wallet, then slide said wallet into his slacks as we rose from the table, I'd made an impulsive, split decision, and I wasn't going back.

So, I let Dawson show me out, let him walk me to his truck, stilling my breath as best I could.

When we got to the truck, he moved to open my door but I stopped him.

Realistically, he'd drive me home, forget about this date-not-date like he forgot about me that first time we met, after we'd flirted.

We'd go back to life as normal—working together, aggravating one another, hiding our true feelings. And I just... didn't want to go back to that.

It's now or never, Nolan.

If you want things to change, change them.

I'd never been more sure of anything in my life.

"Nolan, what—"

I didn't think twice about doing what I'd wanted to do for two years, what I'd wanted to do since that night in M's Place, under his spell, what I wished I had done when we were standing in his brother's front yard.

I pulled Dawson Richards into me and I pressed my lips to his. He startled for a moment, clearly surprised by my sudden boldness, but only for a split second. Then he relaxed in my hold, setting his warm palm on my hip, tugging me closer, his lips moving unhurriedly against mine.

A deep, satisfied groan escaped my throat as his tongue breached my lips. With both hands on my hips, he pulled me tight against him; so tight I could feel his hardness against my own.

I ran my hands up his neck, letting my fingertips play with the edges of his soft hair, and I lived in that kiss for a hundred years.

Because no one had ever kissed me the way Dawson kissed me.

He broke away, and my lips felt swollen and warm from his fiery kiss, longing to be caressed once more.

I think that was when I knew nothing would ever be the same again, and on some deeper level, I knew it was the beginning of something so much greater than I'd ever expected.

But I couldn't process all of that amidst the alcohol infusing my brain.

"Fucking brat," he said with a laugh. "I said, wait till we get home. I told you, good boys get—"

I couldn't help but smile at his words.

"Maybe I don't want to be rewarded, Dawson," I said with a giggle of my own as I boldly went where I'd never gone before. "Maybe I want to be punished instead."

It was Dawson's turn to blush, and I took much pride in that.

He slid his hands down my side, licking his lips as he implored me with his gaze.

"Get. In. The. Car," he said sternly, and I wanted to argue.

To fight him, to instigate him.

It was second nature to me, but I also didn't want to piss him off and make him regret this entire night, so for once, I did as I was told. I climbed into the car, but I didn't miss as Dawson tugged at the tent he'd pitched in his pants before he scrambled into the driver's seat.

I watched as he took a deep breath, his hands tight on the steering wheel as if he was trying to find his own confidence, or his own way out of a deep, dark place.

Back to reality.

He turned the car on, flashing me a look when Metallica came on over the radio.

"I told you, if you were good you could pick the music," he said with a smirk.

"And I am a man of my word, as you know, so go ahead, champ. Have at it."

I smugly smiled, feeling like the truck was only slightly spinning, but I wasn't sure if that was because of the alcohol, or because the way Dawson was looking at me was making me seriously debate going full bad boy and straddling his lap right here.

My desires, my thoughts, my actions... everything was a hazy blur stirring within me like some cyclone.

But I managed to keep from falling apart at the seams, languidly moving forward to gently twist the knob until I'd found a station I liked, which was playing my favorite song. *Hot Blooded.*

Dawson shot me a look as he pulled out of the parking lot, shaking his head as I hummed along and murmured the words to myself. At least, I thought I was singing to myself.

The entire ride home was like that. Both of us singing along to the radio like two teenagers out late on a school night.

And I'd never felt so... free.

So unequivocally *me.*

I'd spent the majority of my life on the sidelines. By myself. My mother always said it was because I was shy, but the reality was I just wasn't comfortable being my awkward self around most people. The world expected you to be a certain way, it classified you based on what you liked, the job you did, and the things you surrounded yourself with. I knew when people looked at me what they saw, the person they'd decided I was, and quite frankly, I didn't see the point in trying to live up to their ideals and expectations, and I didn't want to disappoint anyone. So, I just... didn't open up.

But something about Dawson made me feel like for the first time, it was okay to open up. It was okay to be *me.*

The me who likes to bust out into song like it's an episode of Carpool Karaoke, the me who is sarcastic, the me who is relaxed and fun, and not wound up tighter than an Egyptian mummy most of the time.

I'd barely even noticed when Dawson parked the car at the Towers. Only when the music stopped did I realize we'd been singing and laughing for nearly thirty minutes.

We both sat there in silence for a long moment, and finally, I decided to speak.

"I had... a really great time tonight," I said, not wanting this to end.

I wanted more nights where I felt alive like I did with Dawson.

Dawson moved closer to me, turning to face me. "Me too," he said softly, his gaze roving over me, before settling on my lips.

I scooted closer to him, until our thighs were brushing against one another.

"Dawson, I—"

It was my turn to be surprised, when Dawson reached out, setting his palm against my neck as he pulled me closer, popping one of my buttons as he slid his hand beneath my collar. I shifted my weight until I was practically in his lap. His lips moved against mine with a hunger that echoed my own, and I melted into him like an ice cube on the sidewalk on the Fourth of July.

"Fuck..." I groaned as his tongue slipped into my mouth again, my cock springing back to life.

Instinct took over, and I shifted my weight over his lap, straddling his lap with my thighs. My ass hit the steering wheel, but I didn't care.

Dawson moved his seat back a hair to

give me room, but I didn't want room. I wanted to be as close to Dawson as I could get.

Dawson groaned in my mouth as I ground my rigid erection against his, both loving the friction and hating the barriers between us. My head was spinning.

"Nolan..." he purred, my name on his tongue stronger than any drink I'd ever had. His hand slid up my neck, fingers grasping at my hair with a tight grip, causing my cock to throb. Instinctively, I ground myself against him, needing to feel the friction.

His hands slid down my body in a rushed motion, over my hips, resting on my ass as I let my lips brush his jaw before landing over his neck. I could feel his pulse against my tongue as I licked his skin. His fingers squeezed my ass with a force that had it not been for clothes, would have left a mark. Dawson's touch was full of fire, and I wanted to burn within it.

"Fucking hell... Nolan—"

I stifled his words with my mouth, driven by need, by desire.

Two years.

I'd been dreaming of this man for two

years, fantasizing about this cock for two years.

I didn't want to stop. I didn't want this perfect night to end.

Dawson thrust his hips upward, the motion causing his hardness to slide against mine through our slacks, and I moaned in response, already feeling a wet spot forming in my boxers.

I slid my hands down his chest to his waistband, my fingers ready to claim my prize.

Dawson's hand stopped me, which was like a splash of cold water.

"I think... I think we need..." His breath was coming in rapidly, and I could hear the lust in it, but already my nerves were shot as I realized what was happening.

I'd miscalculated. I was wrong.

Dawson didn't want this.

He didn't want *me.*

"I think we need to slow down."

And just like that, my dreams were shattered.

CHAPTER SIXTEEN

Dawson

IT TOOK EVERY ounce of concentration, every bit of willpower I had, to tell Nolan to stop.

Because I didn't want him to stop.

Fucking hell, I wanted to unearth more of the Nolan I'd seen tonight. The one who wasn't *anything* like I thought he was. The one who blushed constantly at my flirtations, who sang the best karaoke, who knew when to be playful and when to be serious. Who was still a pain in my ass, but was now adding a whole new sort of pain.

When he kissed me outside the restaurant, I was surprised, but mostly because up until that point I didn't think he was into... me. Not like I was slowly becoming into him.

When he kissed me outside the restaurant, his tongue sliding against mine, his dick rubbing against mine, I knew I was a goner. Nolan Harding had blazed through me like a five alarm fire, and I loved it. I wanted more of it.

Which is probably why I had let things get this far to begin with. It was easier to pretend at Sedona that we weren't... us. That we were some beautiful couple on a date, enjoying one another.

But outside home, outside the Towers, reality waited for me.

Nolan wasn't just some hot guy I wanted to take back to my apartment and suck off.

He was my co-worker. He was in charge of my brother's claim.

And he's probably at least a little drunk, and might regret this come tomorrow morning.

I didn't want to be a regret. I wanted to see Nolan again, and not in the capacity I'd been used to.

I wanted *him.*

So, I knew I had to do things right this

time. I had to take my time. Show Nolan that he was worth more than just some truck fuck.

The pain and sadness that registered on his face at my words damn near fucking killed me.

"I'm so sorry. I—" Nolan scrambled off of my lap, leaving my aching boner on full display, the prevalent need to come ebbing in every part of my body.

I leaned my head back against the headrest, closing my eyes as I stilled my breath, grabbing myself to try and stifle my erection. But it was no use, and I was far too sensitive from all of Nolan's dirty grinding, and I came the minute I grabbed myself.

Fuck... I breathed through my ruptured orgasm, the sound of the door slamming pulling me back to the here and now. I adjusted myself as I jumped out of the car, chasing after Nolan when I felt like I needed an eight hour nap.

I don't think I've come in my pants from fucking frotting since I was a damn teen!

"Nolan, wait!" I yelled as he stomped across the parking lot like a petulant child. I jogged to catch up to him, noting the tension in his shoulders. I reached out, grabbing his shoulder, turning him to look at me, and I could see the fire in his eyes.

"Don't," he bit out. "Just... don't make this worse."

"Nolan..." I pleaded as he opened the door, heading for the elevator. I followed him like a lamb to the slaughter.

The elevator dinged and we both tried to go in at once, colliding with one another. I motioned for him to go in first, and he huffed in annoyance. When the elevator closed, Nolan stood there with his arms crossed, refusing to look at me.

"Would you just look at me?" I hissed breathlessly.

"I can't," he said as the elevator opened on his floor. "I'll be fine. Just, let me go."

His words were like ice, and I knew he wouldn't be. Whoever had burned this man before me left some deep wounds. That I was sure of.

My insides ached to soothe him, soothe whatever fear or bullshit he was feeding himself. I needed him to understand that he deserved more.

We deserved more.

I couldn't let him go. So, I ran out of the elevator until I got to his apartment, breathing heavily as he stood in front of his door, keys in hand.

"Nolan, just listen to me, damn it!" I barked, not caring about the volume of my voice. He turned to me with glassy eyes.

"It's not that I don't want to, I do, I just—"

"What? It's not you, it's me? Really, Dawson?" Nolan bit out, his tongue flicking out over his lips as he narrowed his wet gaze at me. He was trying to be tough, but I could see the reality of his emotional state clear as day.

My rejection had hurt him.

I'd fucked up.

I stepped closer, reaching out to touch him because I too, was a glutton for punishment. I expected him to push me away but instead, his shoulders loosened, his eyes gazing up at me with sadness and inebriation.

"It's not you..." I said, the words somehow so clear in my mind, but so difficult to say. So I chose another route. I pulled him close, kissing him once more.

Nolan sunk into my kiss like I was the air he needed to breathe, making my heart race. He broke away, his eyes full of tears.

I pulled him into my arms, wrapping them around him like he was a damn life preserver and I was drowning.

Because in a way, I was. We both were.

Drowning in our own personal hell, in denial.

Nolan's hand settled on my hip as he brushed his face against my shirt.

"Why won't you let me be the good guy for once?" I asked, my voice barely a whisper.

I pulled away, looking at his face, at the pain in his expression.

Pain I caused.

Fuck, how do I make this right?

Nolan turned away from me for a moment, his dark lashes standing out against his pale skin, the sheen of his black frames catching the light from above in the hallway.

He turned back to me, his voice pained.

"Because that's my job, Dawson. To be the good guy. You're *supposed* to the bad guy," he chortled.

"What do you mean?" I asked, feeling my own heart break at his words.

Was that how he saw me?

Truly?

As some Bond villain?

Nolan stepped forward an inch, closing the distance between us that had formed. "You're supposed to fucking ruin me," he said, tears falling down his pale cheeks, his voice dark and full of things that made my cock twitch again.

Made my blood hot.

Nolan said the words, but I felt them in my core.

He wanted to burn.

He wanted me in the worst way, and the reality of that notion scared me more than anything else.

I slid my hands through his soft, dark hair, staring back at his beautiful, tear-stained face, and I felt on the edge of a cliff.

And that was when I decided to jump.

A part of me knew he may not remember this conversation in the morning, but if he did... I hoped he'd at least respect me for it.

"If you want this..." I breathed heavily, stroking the wet streaks on his cheek with my thumb. "If you want *me*," I started. "Then you can have me. But not like this," I whispered, planting a kiss on his forehead.

Nolan pushed me away.

"Whatever, Dawson," he said as he unlocked his door, and I watched him disappear, leaving me and my heart in ruin.

I only prayed that we could rebuild what I'd broken.

CHAPTER SEVENTEEN

Nolan

I WOKE UP with a pounding headache, a dry mouth, and an overbearing need to piss. The sunlight filtered in through my window, and it was blindingly bright as I shielded my eyes from it.

I groaned as reality set in, memories of the prior night playing over in my mind like a movie. Dawson and I... We kissed.

Fuck, I kissed him!

The memory of Dawson relaxing into me, of his warm lips against mine, made my entire body flush with heat.

I'd had probably a little more than I could handle in the liquor department, but to be fair, those drinks didn't even taste like they had alcohol in them at all. It was like sucking down a Capri Sun. But the throbbing pain in my head told me those sweet, fizzy drinks packed quite a punch.

I leaned back in my bed, running my hand over my eyes as I let the hazy memories surface, as I tried to hold on to what had happened, how things had transpired.

Though I remembered kissing Dawson, everything else seemed rather vague and blurry. As if one moment bled into the next, and all I could remember was the feel of his lips on mine, of his cock against mine.

Fuck!

I want you to ruin me.

The words surfaced in my brain, and even though I was alone with no one to witness my mortification, I blushed what I would have guessed was a deep scarlet from the way my entire body heated at the memory.

Of me being pissed off because we...

Were making out in his truck!

And I told him that?

That I wanted *him to fucking ruin me?*

I groaned miserably as I grabbed the

pillow next to me, feeling a slight panic attack coming on.

Breathe, Nolan, it's fine.

You can blame it on the fizzy bubbly drinks... maybe he doesn't remember anyway... or...

Honestly, I wasn't sure I *could* blame it all on the alcohol. That may have accounted for my loose lips, but it wasn't like I was lying about what I said. I *did* want Dawson to ruin me. I wanted him to destroy me in more ways than one, and then build me back up from total destruction.

The memory of his fingers gripping my ass resurfaced, only causing more of a mixture of pain and embarrassment meddled with lust and desire.

I am so fucked up.

I wanted him to forget my momentary lapse of judgment, my embarrassing, desperate attempt to lull him into my apartment and live out my stupid fantasy.

After all, I *was* practically throwing myself at him.

And his answer had been very clear, because here I was, awake and alone.

But I didn't have time to process such things. Duty called, after all. I swung my legs over the side of the bed and planted my feet on the carpet as I tried to stabilize my breath.

Of two things I was absolutely certain. One, that Dawson had kissed me back.

Which changed *everything.*

But the second thing I knew was that despite the fact he seemed into it, he left me alone on my doorstep, pissed off, horny, and rejected. He just... left.

Because I wasn't good enough.

Because I'd upset the delicate balance of the tightrope between us.

Because he wanted to be a good guy.

Maybe I'd ruined everything.

I felt a sting of guilt, but it would have to be short-lived, because not ten seconds later my phone was ringing, louder than it probably should have been.

I fumbled with my phone on the nightstand, knocking over a box of tissues as I squinted to see the screen.

Karla calling.

Great, just who I wanted to hear from at seven thirty in the morning when I was hungover.

"Hello?" I answered groggily.

"Morning sleepyhead," Karla said in a tone that was much too chipper for my liking.

"I could have used five more minutes..." I groaned as I slowly ambled my way across the floor to the hallway and down to the bathroom.

"I bet. You sound like shit. You're not sick, are you?" she asked, her tone changing to one of concern.

I easily slid my cock out of my boxers, relieving myself while I tried to focus.

"I wish," I mumbled. "But no."

"Techs should be wrapping up this morning, so you're good to come back in the office this afternoon. You should be all recharged and ready to go," she said.

"Great," I touted as I tucked myself back in my boxers.

"Sounds great, hun. See you this afternoon!" she said, her voice filled with excitement.

I'm glad one of us is in a good mood.

CHAPTER EIGHTEEN

Nolan

I PULLED UP to the Breisinger building like a functional human being, despite feeling the exact opposite. I clutched my iced coffee, forcing a smile as I walked through the doors past Brittany, our receptionist.

"Afternoon, Mr. Harding," she said with faked enthusiasm that I couldn't even muster at the moment.

"Afternoon, Britt," I said as I headed for my office.

"Regional called about the Bradish claim."

I stopped dead in my tracks.

Bradish... That would be Dawson's

brother... What could Regional possibly want?

"Did they say what it was about?" I asked, already on edge. We rarely got calls from the big guys, they usually left us alone as long as we closed our claims and met our goals, and I'd only gotten a call from them once, regarding one of Dawson's claims when I'd first started. It had been a clear misunderstanding. Something Dawson noted that wasn't listed under the right subset or something. I'd learned after that call to double check *everything* submitted by Dawson and his crew, if only because I didn't want any oversights and to have Regional breathing down my neck.

Britt shrugged. "Not really, just said they wanted you to call them back when you got in."

I nodded, my grip around my ice coffee tightening as I mustered a half-smile. Maybe when I didn't have a pounding headache I could pretend, but not today.

"Thanks, Britt," I said as I made a beeline for my door, doing my best to evade Karla's office door, which was open. I didn't dislike my boss, but sometimes she had a tendency to want to gossip and chitchat when I wanted nothing to do with the insider gossip on Jasper Springs's residents.

I tried to stay out of the drama, thank you very much.

With a hefty amount of luck, I managed to squeeze past her door while she was otherwise engaged in something at her computer, taking refuge in my office and immediately shutting the door.

Flopping down in my chair, I let out a heavy breath.

Okay, Nolan, just take it easy. You don't know it's anything bad...

I set up at my desk, focusing on my breath.

Here goes nothing.

CHAPTER NINETEEN

Nolan

I LET OUT a sigh of frustration as I hung up the phone. Apparently, the files I'd sent electronically had gotten all fucked up, and I needed to re-evaluate the claim with brand new photos, a brand new report... and video of the location and business.

Fuck me.

Just as I contemplated crumbling into a million pieces, Karla's voice cut through my disdain.

"Guess you heard from Regional?" she asked, crossing her arms.

"Yeah," I mumbled.

"You're not the only one. Lex and

Stacey also have to go back out and do re-evals. Seems whatever was going on with our computers, you all had some serious damage to your files. I asked the techs about it and they said with the new upgrades it likely won't happen again, and it was a fluke."

Yeah, a fluke that just had to happen on the worst day of my life.

"I literally just got here..."

Karla softened her gaze. "You okay? You seem... grouchy. More so than usual," she pried, no doubt looking for gossip, and a part of me wanted to talk. But another knew whatever I had to process or say would be better left in my own mind than to be aired out for Jasper Springs's Blair Waldorf.

"I'm fine, just... I need to get caught up here. You know, get back to work..."

Karla's gaze steadied as she squinted, sizing me up.

If she could tell I was lying, she didn't show it. Instead, she nodded and said, "Okay, Nolan. But I'm watching you." She pointed between us sarcastically.

"Yeah, yeah, I get it," I said as my email started to sound, the whistle of work calling me. I stared at my inbox, a part of me hoping to see an email from Dawson. He loved to blow up my inbox with insults and nitpicks about the claims of his I'd checked.

But my shoulders sunk when I saw nothing. Nothing from anyone other than Karla and Regional, anyway.

Certainly not anything from Dawson Richards.

I let out a breath, leaning back in my chair. I wanted to reach out, apologize for what an ass I'd been... but I also didn't want to appear overbearing, or cliché.

I've never done this before, or I don't usually act like this is definitely cliché. Worse, it's juvenile. I'm a twenty-eight year old adult. I've certainly done this before.

Enough to know that it was probably better I leave Dawson alone for a day or two, let things smooth over, let him have time to forget what happened. Forget me.

And maybe I should forget him too. Be happy we'd had a decent time before I blew everything to smithereens.

I took another long pull of my iced coffee, checking the clock on my computer screen. Four more hours left in this day, surely I could manage that.

CHAPTER TWENTY

Nolan

I STARED AT my phone, at the text thread that remained empty. He hadn't texted me, and I hadn't made a move to do so either. Instead, I'd only stared at that blank text bubble all day as if I could magically wield the words on screen. Words that would somehow fix this, erase my embarrassing behavior, and put us back to square one.

In the woods.

Where I could lose the race, and the chance to have ever been so close to such perfection. Where I could exist not knowing how good his lips tasted against mine.

I set the phone down on the bar as I pushed away for a moment, grabbing my beer as I glanced around the room.

I didn't come to M's Place often, but after feeling like shit all day at work about everything—my botched date, my job, my life in general—I didn't want to go home.

When I found myself in front of the bar, I didn't question it. It wasn't the same as being with someone, or talking to someone, but it beat going home alone to wallow.

Wallowing at a bar is what normal people do anyway, isn't it?

That was when I saw him.

With someone else.

Instinctively, I felt a sting of jealousy, mixed with sadness and anger.

I knew I didn't have a claim on Dawson, that he was free to do whatever he wanted with whoever he wanted, but even knowing that I couldn't help it.

Especially when the guy he was with was absolutely gorgeous compared to me. Toned, defined form, golden blond hair... He looked like a Calvin Klein model or something. Not to mention the two seemed pretty comfortable with one another, smiling and laughing.

Which only made me feel worse.

How could I have been so stupid?

Dawson had said he hadn't been on a date in awhile, and I wanted to believe him, but was I that easily played?

He probably told *all* the guys that. It was probably part of his charm or act.

I drained the last of my beer, feeling like I needed to get out of the place.

Away from the sight of Dawson with Mr. Perfect.

So, I threw my cash on the counter, with a nice tip of course, considering I'd only bought the one drink, but that was all I needed, and honestly, after seeing Dawson with his date, it was all I could stomach.

CHAPTER TWENTY-ONE

Dawson

OF ALL THE days to be slow, today was the slowest.

I leaned my head back against the couch in the living room upstairs in the firehouse, fighting to concentrate on anything except the previous night.

On the memory of my embarrassing moment.

Granted, Nolan had no idea all his grinding had caused me to explode in such a fashion, and I wasn't about to tell him that little tidbit. I'd take that to my fucking grave.

But the fact of the matter was, I knew there was absolutely no way I'd be able to look at Nolan the same again.

Not after he'd kissed me, after he'd wriggled his way onto my lap and into my damn heart like he had.

I wanted to text him. All day I thought about it, but I didn't want to seem too forward. I wasn't sure how much he remembered, if he remembered pinning me beneath him in my truck and making my damn head spin, or if he was hungover as shit and wanted to be left alone. I knew I hated to be bothered when I drank a bit too much, when I was hungover as shit.

No, I knew I needed to give Nolan space, and I didn't want to appear... clingy.

Even though I'm dying to know his thoughts, if he remembers what happened.

If he regrets what happened.

I hated leaving Nolan like I had. I'd wanted to give into temptation, wanted to *ruin* him as he requested, but I also wanted more... I knew I had to tread carefully because the last thing I wanted was to create problems for either of us at work.

Firehouse gossip spreads fast too.

The clock chimed on three, waking me

from my spell of self-loathing just as my phone buzzed.

In an awful moment of weakness earlier, I'd texted the one person who knew me better than most, because I knew I needed to talk or I'd end up doing something I regretted.

Like send a string of text messages that made me appear like a level six stalker.

I needed to get things out in the open, to be able to process what had happened and how I could fix things, and there wasn't anyone I trusted more with my secrets than Cade.

Mitch was a great friend, don't get me wrong, but his emotional capacity was only a smidge higher than an amoeba.

The man was about as anti-romance as you could get. If I needed help moving something, or new social media photos, or even to borrow twenty bucks, Mitch was the guy to ask. But if I needed advice on dick and all things centered around the dick... I was better asking a hopeless romantic like Cade.

I'd half expected him to blow me off, being as he and his new boyfriend were practically attached at the hip, and I was pleasantly surprised when he answered my angsty, emo-kid text with, '*Sure, let's meet up at M's this evening and talk about it. What time you off?*'

The instant relief that poured over me should have been embarrassing had I not felt the stress of everything melt almost immediately.

I wasn't sure what the right thing to do was, but I knew at least if I talked things out with my best friend, he'd steer me in the right direction.

CHAPTER TWENTY-TWO

Dawson

WHEN I WALKED into M's Place at five-thirty, Cade was already waiting. His bright blue eyes caught mine from across the room, and I didn't miss the smile. He'd had a rough year, before Weston showed up in town to sweep him off his feet like some knight in fine tailored armor, riding his trusty BMW steed, and I had to admit, happiness looked good on him.

I wish I could have that too.

"Hey," he said as he reached out to hug me.

I hugged him back, already feeling a little better. I'd never been an emotional person. In fact, I'd always been pretty clear-headed and level when it came to tough situations, knowing how to rein my feelings in to prevent a bigger issue, but it seemed like lately I was losing my ability to not give a fuck.

My walls were crumbling around me and I knew why. I just didn't want to admit it out loud.

"Hey," I said as we broke apart our hug and took our seats.

"So, tell me about this guy that's got you all—" He whistled, a slow smile spreading across his face.

I sighed.

Well, it's now or never.

"He's not just... some guy. Cade, he's..." I struggled to find my words, but true to his nature, Cade was as patient as a saint with me.

"It's... Nolan."

"Nolan riding your ass again at work? I told you—"

"No, Cade. The guy that's... It's Nolan. We sort of... ran into each other on the trail at the Towers, and I sort of made a bet with him, and he won, and we sort of went on a date, but it wasn't supposed to be a date, and then we kissed, and started making out in my truck, and I lost it, and he ran off, and…"

"Slow down, Dawson. One thing at a time…" Cade said, his eyebrows furrowing in concentration.

"I just, uh… I think somehow I may have fucked shit up, and I'm not sure what to do."

Cade smiled, shaking his head. "I knew it. You got it bad, huh?" he said slyly.

On instinct, I balked at his comment. After all, I'd prided myself for years on my carefree personality, the guy who just had fun without getting too involved in anything remotely serious.

It was still strange despite how I felt inside, to hear someone else say it out loud.

"I wouldn't go that far, I—"

Cade's shoulders loosened as he sat back in his chair, eyeing me like a teacher eyes the kid in class who screamed when they weren't supposed to.

"Dawson. It's me. You can be honest."

"It's complicated," I said, hating how cliché I sounded.

"It always is," Cade said as the waiter finally came by to take our order.

I opted for a beer and a basket of hot wings, while Cade opted for a spiked seltzer and some fried pickles. He briefly checked his phone, a smile gracing his lips, and I almost rolled my eyes.

"Prince Charming whispering sweet nothings in your ear again?"

Cade set his phone down, smirking. "Actually, he said he's getting out of work early, and asked if he could join us?"

I wanted to be pissed. Really, I did, but seeing the way Cade lit up when he talked about the man made it hard to say no.

"Of course, the more the merrier," I said with a half-smile. It wasn't that I didn't like Weston, or that I felt like I deserved this alone time with Cade and selfishly wanted to keep it that way. I wanted to be supportive, not just for my friend, but also because I felt some sort of intrinsic responsibility for setting them up in the first place, for telling Cade to go after what he wanted—Weston—just like he was sitting here listening to me drone on about a very attractive complication of my own.

Besides, Weston seemed like a decent guy. Not that that meant I was going to tell him all my secrets and have a slumber party with the guy any time soon, but I wasn't about to say no to another drinking buddy and the man who clearly made my best friend happy.

Cade tapped out his response on his phone before looking back at me with his know-it-all stare.

"All I'm saying is, if you like him, you should be honest."

"It's not that easy..." I said, letting out a defeated sigh.

Cade pressed. "Why not? What's so hard about—"

"Well, for starters, we work together."

Cade raised an eyebrow in surprise. "And? When has something like that ever been an issue for you? You dated Vance, and he worked for Breisinger."

Just the mention of my ex, made me stiffen. I'd been a different person then, and I knew even though it shouldn't bother me that Nolan had replaced my ex at his job, it felt like in a way he was angling to replace him in my heart too. But that was stupid, and it wasn't like Nolan knew about my internal grudge.

However, as Cade said the words, I wondered if maybe that's what I wanted.

For Nolan to heal my broken heart.

"It's just…"

"Complicated, I know," Cade snarked.

"Dawson, you've been an upfront guy as long as I have known you. You don't mince words, and you're honest to a fault. Hell, it was one of the things that *I* was drawn to, when I met you. You're bold and confident, and that's sexy as hell. So, what exactly are you afraid of losing if you come clean with Nolan, because we both know it's not like you're going to lose your job or anything."

Cade was right, but I just didn't want to admit that.

Thankfully, I didn't have to because the waiter came with my basket of wings and Cade's pickles and the rest of the conversation died in favor of our sustenance.

I'd just finished the last hot wing when I noticed a familiar head of dark hair at the bar, thick, black glasses glinting in the light like the north star in the woods.

My pulse heated immediately, my stomach doing flips—although, I couldn't be certain if that was in part to the food I'd just inhaled, or if it was because of the attractive nerd of my damn dreams.

Mr. Complicated.

Suddenly, my agonizing over texts seemed crazy when he was just within my reach. Maybe if we could talk, I could tell him how sorry I was that I upset him. Maybe we could have a do-over.

An actual date where we were both on the same page.

"I'll be right back," I said, not able to resist the pull of Nolan Harding even if my damn life depended on it.

I wandered through the crowd until I came up to him, setting my hand on his oblivious shoulder as he rose from his seat at the bar.

"Hey," I said nervously.

Nolan turned around quickly, his eyes widening in surprise. "Hey..." he said, swallowing harshly, his gaze turning from surprised to hurt.

"I wanted to text you earlier, but I wasn't sure how you were feeling after—"

"Really? Could have fooled me," Nolan growled.

Excuse me?

"I'm not sure..."

"You know, I get it. I'm not everyone's cup of tea, but my mother always said I'd be someone's shot of whiskey. Guess I wasn't yours though, was I?" he said as he turned away.

Oh fuck no.

I grabbed him by the shoulder, this time much more harshly.

"What the fuck? Where is this coming from, I thought—"

"You thought what, Dawson? That I was fun to dick around for a night, but not enough to call the next day? Or were you too busy planning your next date with Apollo over there?" he said as he brushed me off, stomping off toward the bathroom.

And like the lovesick fool I was, I ran after him, angered and placated by his sudden bout of jealousy as I realized he must have seen me with Cade and assumed the worst.

"Who? Cade? He's not... I mean we dated once, but it's not like that. Not anymore. He's just a friend, I promise, I—"

"Save your excuses for someone who cares, Dawson," he retorted as he headed for the exit.

But I wouldn't let him get that far. Not until I said what I needed to, to clear the air, but also... because the words were on the tip of my tongue and I knew if I didn't do it then, I'd lose my nerve.

And I'd lose Nolan forever.

I blocked his exit with my body, causing him to crash up against me. He stumbled with a growl.

"Dawson get out of my way, I—"

"No," I said as I challenged his space, backing him up against the wall. "I've had enough of your mouth. It's *my* turn to talk, champ."

Nolan gazed up at me with fire in his eyes, his lips pursed into a thin line, but he didn't move a muscle.

Because I was a glutton for punishment as much as I was for laying it on thick, and because it was impossible to stand in front of this man who made my entire body heat with passion and anger, I reached my hand out, settling my palm against his neck. I tightened my fingers around the back of his head, his silky hair tickling the back of my knuckles.

There was so much I wanted to say. I knew what I *should* have said.

But instead, I found myself rising to Nolan's anger, his jealousy, blossoming like an angry lotus.

How dare he insinuate I don't give a

shit about him or what happened!

"You are being a fucking brat right now," I said, my voice much darker than I intended.

Nolan opened his mouth to speak, but he never would get the words out.

Because the moment his luscious lips parted, I claimed them with mine, pouring my pent up frustration, my anger, and my wildy catching feelings into that kiss.

I expected him to fight me, to make some snide comment or get cocky, but instead, Nolan fell back against the wall, his hand snaking its way up my neck, pulling me closer.

And into his gravity I fell, like a damn meteorite crashing to earth.

Nolan Harding was the sun at the center of my universe and I had no idea how to process that, especially at that moment.

But *damn it,* I was going to try.

I pulled away, relishing in his heavy, heated breath, in the feel of his body pressed against mine.

"I loathe your fucking attitude," I snarled.

Nolan's fingers gripped the edges of my hair as I gazed at his delicious lips, swollen from our heated kiss.

And then he said the magic words.

The words that would undoubtedly change both our lives forever.

"Then fucking do something about it, Dawson," he said calmly as he broke free from my grasp, sliding out the door like a thief in the night, leaving me alone in the dark to realize that this situation was more than just complicated.

Because without a doubt, I was falling in love with Nolan.

CHAPTER TWENTY-THREE

Nolan

MY LUNGS ACHED, and the room smelled like burnt toast. My dreams disintegrated into ash as I awoke to a thick, dense cloud of smoke blanketing me and the sound of alarms blared through my groggy consciousness.

But it took all of mere seconds for me to understand what was happening.

Fire.

Something had happened, and I was in danger, and my adrenaline immediately spiked. I didn't think twice about throwing my legs over the side of my bed, grabbing my glasses and phone from the bedside table, and dropping to the ground.

The heat from the fire ebbed like a pulse, but I didn't see any flames in my bedroom as I army crawled across the floor. Though the smoke made it hard as hell to see, and my lungs hurt to breathe, I knew I had to keep going if I wanted to make it out of there alive.

Every ounce of my being focused on finding my way to the door.

When I finally did, I fought to push it open, and made my way out into the hall, my vision still blurry from the smoke. But what I could see was tenants evacuating, firemen running into doors, and the sound of the blaring alarms made it hard to concentrate. I tried to stand, stumbling as I clutched the wall and tried to clear my vision.

Just a few more steps...

"Nolan!" a familiar voice cut through the confusion as I tried to focus my eyesight on where it was coming from. I coughed so hard my stomach twisted.

"Fuck, Nolan, it's okay, you're okay..." Steady, strong arms pulled me in, giving me the support I needed to stand. Through my smoke-clouded vision I could make out Dawson's perfect face, his copper eyes full of concern.

"Dawson... What..."

"Come on, champ, let's get you somewhere safe," he said, his voice stern and commanding.

I tried to move, but my legs felt like deadweight and I stumbled as I tried to follow his lead. "I can't... I..." My words were choked and labored, and I could barely process what had happened.

I felt my body being swept up off the ground like I was nothing more than a ragdoll. My head fell against a soft, damp shirt that smelled like cedar and spice, the fabric warm to my cheek, and like a confused, dazed idiot, I burrowed into it seeking its warmth and safety.

"It's okay, I got you. You're gonna be okay, I promise." Dawson's voice faltered only a moment, but it soothed me nonetheless.

Then darkness came, and took with it the smell of smoke, the heat of fire, and all the things I'd thought mattered, but in this moment knew they were miniscule.

I could feel my body being moved as I clutched my phone to my chest. The warmth and safety of Dawson's arms left me, and I hated it. I wanted to crawl into his hold and never leave.

"The paramedics need to check you out, okay? I'll be back, I promise," he said calmly, brushing my hair back from my face.

My eyelids fluttered as he came into my vision, the chill air kissing my skin. He was truly the most beautiful thing I'd ever seen, soot all over his face, standing there in a damp, white shirt, against the glow of a fire and smoke.

My hero.

I reached for him, to tell him I was sorry. I was wrong. For what, I wasn't sure, but the need to apologize was overwhelming.

Dawson only took my hand for a moment, nodding at me. "Promise," he said before he let me go, and I watched my hero disappear into the smoke without a moment's hesitation.

My heart ached as I watched him boldly do what it was he did every day.

The paramedics put an oxygen mask on me, taking my pulse, checking me over. Someone mentioned something or other about my rapid heartbeat, about my vitals, but it was all white noise in comparison to the realization that I was alive, and I was okay, and that Dawson had saved my life.

And I prayed to whatever God would listen to me that he would come back to me, because in that moment, I'd never seen anything clearer.

I was falling in love with Dawson Richards, and the thought of losing him—to a fire, or even to my own selfish, self-sabotaging behavior—terrified me.

I watched in silent horror as the firemen evacuated the second floor, and the first, where apparently the fire had started, according to the chatter of the paramedics.

And when the fire had been cleansed, when the threat had been diminished, I waited for what felt like an eternity as my vision returned, my breathing evened out.

"Can I make a phone call?" I asked, once I was free of my oxygen mask, my breathing stable. The paramedic shrugged.

"Probably a good idea to call someone you can stay with for awhile until this mess is sorted."

His words settled on me, and I realized he was right. There was no way I was getting back in my apartment tonight, given there would need to be an official claim for the building, not to mention individual tenant's claims about the damages incurred... including my own.

But I didn't really know anyone in Jasper Springs, and Allie wasn't close by. Still, I felt I should call her and let her know what happened. Maybe I could take up residence in the Paradise Hotel for a little while.

I checked the time; it was around two in the morning. I hated to wake her but...

In my wandering, I'd accidentally hit the Facetime button instead of call, and barely had time to register what happened before she accepted the call.

"Nolan, are you okay?" she said immediately, knowing a two am call from me was probably the worst. For goodness' sake, I was in bed by ten thirty most nights.

"I..." My voice caught as the words fell out. "I am now. There was a fire in my building, and..."

"Oh my God!" Allie said as she sat up in bed.

"I made it out okay, and then Dawson..."

The sight of Dawson walking toward

me, decked out in his yellow fire suit and hat made my heart stop and my voice die on the wind.

He looked so badass it would have been impossible *not* to fall in love with the man.

"Nolan... Nolan!" Allie yelled.

I turned the phone in his direction absentmindedly, and Allie gasped.

"Is that..."

"The man who saved my life, yeah," I said softly.

"Oh, Nolan..." Allie tutted.

"I'm... going to have to call you back, Allie," I said.

"Nolan..."

"I'm okay, I promise. I just... I'll call you with any updates, okay?" I said as Dawson came closer, just a few feet away now.

"Fine. But I'm holding you to that!" she blurted and I ended our call.

Dawson stopped just inches away from me, his golden gaze roving over me.

"You're okay..." he said, his voice filled with relief, and I felt it through every part of my being.

I nodded dumbly. "Yeah, because of you..." I said.

"This one's good to go, right?" Dawson asked the paramedic beside me.

"Minor smoke inhalation, maybe a little shock, but otherwise, yeah. Vitals are stable."

"Good. Because he's coming with me," Dawson proclaimed.

"I... I need to get over to the Paradise," I said, trying to remember how to speak.

Dawson only shook his head.

"Like hell you are. I ain't letting you out of my sight, champ. You're under my watch until—"

"You don't have to do that," I said as I rubbed my arms. The cold night air was getting to me.

Dawson instinctively pulled off his fireproof jacket, throwing it over my shoulders like the hero he truly was.

"I know, but I want to," he said as he adjusted the jacket, looking down at me. "Let me take care of you, Nolan."

Something about his words made my heart melt, decimated all the anger and the upset, and the unspoken words. Looking up at his amber eyes of fire, I couldn't resist him.

How could I tell him no, when I never wanted to leave his arms or his golden presence?

"Okay," I agreed, my voice shaky as he ran his hand along my back, guiding me toward the building stairs.

"Fire was electrical. Caught in the cafe. Second floor only sustained smoke damage, which is good, and third floors and above are all untouched. Everyone has been evacuated, and arrangements are being made," he said as he coaxed me along, never removing his hand from my back.

"Oh, okay," I said, because I wasn't sure what else to say. I guessed the paramedic was right, I was in shock.

"You can stay with me as long as you need until things get back to normal, okay?" he said as I followed him up three flights of steps and down the hall. I nodded, tugging his jacket closer. It smelled of fire and spice, and I liked it. I liked it a lot, because it made me feel warm and safe.

It made me feel *loved*.

But that was crazy, and I knew that. I blamed it on the shock, because there was no way in hell Dawson was in love with me. The man barely tolerated me, and had downright rejected my advances.

He's just doing his job.

Dawson opened the door for me, and I stepped across the threshold into the darkness once more.

CHAPTER TWENTY-FOUR

Dawson

MY HEART THUDDED away in my chest as the sound of the shower filled the otherwise silent air of my home.

I'd fought plenty of fires in my lifetime, but this one was different. I'd never been in a position where I felt so powerless before.

It was my job to go in and save people, to pull them out of burning buildings and residences, get them the help they needed.

But as I ran with Nolan in my arms, it was the first time I'd felt sincerely panicked, worried that I might have failed.

And if something happened to him, I

wasn't sure I could handle it.

It had taken everything in me to leave him with Jordan and the other paramedics, and focus on my job.

But I prayed that when I returned, he'd be okay. I had to believe he would, because I couldn't stand to think otherwise.

The sight of him, alive and okay, made my damn heart feel like it was going to explode. I knew his apartment would be out of commission for the next couple days until the claims and everything settled, and maybe I offered for him to stay out of a sense of guilt, or maybe I did it because somewhere deep down where I didn't want to admit, I was scared. Scared that I'd almost lost him.

Scared that something could have happened to him and I wouldn't have been able to protect him. It was a weird tug in my chest, the thought and desire to protect this bratty, infuriating, beautiful man.

There was no way I was letting him out of my sight.

Not tonight, not ever.

"Hey," his voice cut through my wandering thoughts, bringing me back to the here and now, reality staring at me with a well-toned chest and a rather delicious Adonis belt poking out of the size too big sweatpants I'd loaned him.

Nolan's hair was still wet from his shower, his dark eyes behind his glasses full of apprehension.

"Wow," I murmured under my breath without warning, heat returning to my body to remind me I was alive, and Nolan was here.

In my apartment, dressed in my sweats, looking like my fantasy come to life.

"I, uh... appreciate your, uh... letting me stay. I promise, I'll figure things out tomorrow. I just—"

I pushed away from my counter, taking my time as I walked across the room, drawn to Nolan Harding like kerosene to a fire.

"You can stay as long as you need," I said as I stopped in front of him. Nolan's gaze searched mine, for what I wasn't sure, but I couldn't help myself in his presence.

Every time I got close to the man, I found it hard to resist touching him, to resist falling into his enchanting spell.

"Dawson, I..."

"Are you hungry?" I asked, pushing some stray strands of hair out of his glasses, watching the way his eyes sparkled in the dim light of my hallway.

"What?" Nolan asked, though his voice was soft, and he didn't break my gaze.

"I said, are you hungry?" I repeated myself, the innate desire to take care of this man overriding the rest of my ill-formed psyche that was losing its last marble.

"I... kind of... I mean..."

"Sit down on the couch," I commanded as I turned away.

"What?" he asked as he followed me, the sound of his bare feet on the tiles echoing in the small space.

"I said, sit down. Take a load off. I'll grab you something," I told him as I headed for my fridge.

"Fine," Nolan grumbled, but he did as I asked.

So, he can listen... when he wants to.

I set about to grabbing the ingredients for the one thing that always made *me* feel better. I wasn't entirely sure it would work for Nolan, but it was worth a shot. I set the chocolate and Nutella spread out, gathered my latest batch of specialty marshmallows from Penn's Bakery, and fished the graham crackers out of the cupboard.

I turned to see Nolan curling up on my couch, noting how good he looked in my clothes. Like he was well and truly *mine.*

I swallowed at the thought of the word. I wasn't the possessive type, and I'd never been. But something about Nolan brought out a side of me I'd never known, and I didn't dislike it.

Not one bit.

I quickly slathered my graham crackers with the equal amounts of chocolate and Nutella spread, taking my time as I assembled my plate of s'mores. It didn't take long until I had four of them done, and I tossed them in the air fryer.

I turned, setting my gaze on Nolan, who was watching me intently.

"Is there anything you don't do?" he asked, his voice edged with sarcasm.

"I..."

"It's like, just when I think I know you... you find some way to keep me guessing."

It was my turn to smile. "I could say the same about you, you know."

"Me?" Nolan's eyes widened and I smirked, noting the blush that crept onto his cheeks made my cock twitch and my heart race.

"Yeah, you. For the last two years, I thought I had you pegged. Then all of a sudden, you show up to bar bingo and get all cocky with me... then you beat me running, and then you—" I swallowed, my words dying in the air as I remembered Nolan and his mouthwatering kiss, his rigid hardness against my own causing me to see stars as I came in my damn pants like a teenager.

How my heart panicked when I saw him in the hallway earlier.

The air fryer dinged, perfectly on cue to break up the tense moment.

"I, uh... hold that thought," I said as I pulled the s'mores out with my fingers quickly to avoid getting burned.

I grabbed the plate and made my way over to the couch, taking a seat next to Nolan. The cushions moved only slightly where I sat, making Nolan slope toward me in the slightest movement.

He looked at my plate with eyes as wide as saucers.

"Air fried s'mores?" he said with a raise

of his eyebrow.

"Whenever I have a shit day, a little chocolate therapy usually does the trick. Unless, of course, you don't like—"

"I like it, Dawson," he said, his dark eyes focused on me intently. Something about his words felt off, like he wanted to say more but thought better of it.

I offered him the first bite, and he took it.

His eyelashes fluttered, and he groaned as he took his bite, the sound going straight to my cock, and I had to cover my own mouth to stifle a groan.

Fuuuuuck.

"Oh man, that's good," he said, licking his lips of the remains of gooey marshmallow and chocolate.

I smiled as I reached for a s'more of my own, letting the warm, smooth sweetness coat my tongue and settle my nerves a bit. I leaned back into my cushions, the motion bringing my shoulder right against Nolan's. I expected him to move away, but he didn't. In fact, he leaned a little closer.

Instinctively, I wanted to wrap my free arm around him, but I also didn't want to ruin this perfect moment.

To my surprise, he shifted his position,

turning toward me. In the light of my apartment, his pale skin took on an almost angelic glow, his dark frames and eyes captivating me like the sucker I truly was in his presence.

God, was he pretty like this. Relaxed, freshly showered, lips begging to be kissed.

Fuck me sideways.

"I need to tell you something," he said with a sigh.

I slowly chewed the remainder of my smore as I nodded, completely dumbfounded under his gaze.

"Well, out with it then," I said as I swallowed the sweetness down my throat.

"I need to apologize," he said as he ran a hand through his dark hair, his eyelashes fluttering, lips pursed in a tight line.

"Apologize for what, Nolan?" I asked as I shifted my position, turning my body to face him. The motion made us both sink into the cushions, our legs brushing one another in a soft collision.

I licked some chocolate off my thumb, watching his nose and cheeks redden as he let out a shaky breath.

"For being a dick earlier tonight, at M's

Place... I..."

I wanted to stop him, tell him it didn't matter. All that mattered now was he was safe, and he was here. With me.

But something told me, that wasn't what I should do, and so I said nothing.

Nolan continued. "I think your asshole tendencies might be rubbing off on me," he said with a nervous laugh.

The sound made me smile, and instinctively I reached out and set my hand on his thigh, patting him with a gesture that was somehow both assuring, and soft all at once.

"You know what I think?" I asked with a smirk.

Nolan raised an eyebrow. "What?" he asked, pulling his pouty bottom lip in between his teeth, causing my cock to twitch again.

"I think you're just a natural brat," I said, my voice much darker than I intended.

Nolan looked back at me in question, chewing his lip. "I—" he started, just as I shook my head, placing a finger on his lips to shut him up.

"It's not a bad thing, Nolan. I kind of... like it. I..."

Nolan's soft lips against my fingertips were warm, igniting a fire in my blood that was hard to ignore.

The words fell out of my mouth without warning. "I kind of like... you."

The weight of those words left me feeling lighter after I'd said them.

Because I understood at that moment the truth they held.

I did like Nolan.

I liked him a whole hell of a lot, and on some deeper level, I needed him to know that. I needed to be clear, and honest, just like Cade had told me to be.

But first, I needed to admit the truth to myself, and that truth was that Nolan Harding was more to me than some thorn in my side, pain in the ass arch nemesis.

He was the match and I was the fuse.

Nolan leaned into my space, the couch creaking just a bit as his motion drew me closer into him, like quicksand.

Nolan reached out a shaky hand, sliding his fingers in my hair softly, gripping as if he were afraid I would disappear at any moment.

Like he was afraid of upsetting the delicate balance of the cliff we were both on.

I slid my hand up and down his thigh, trying to reassure him the best way I knew how that this was what I wanted, because I couldn't speak. I could only focus on feeling him beneath my fingertips, because I didn't want him to disappear either.

I pulled him closer, the position once again putting him in my lap, and Nolan let out a sigh that cut straight through to my heart, my cock, and my feeble Nolan-obsessed brain.

"I kinda like you too, Dawson," he whispered, his breath warm on the edge of my lips, and I didn't wait.

I closed the space between us without warning, tasting his sweet lips and the remains of sticky sugar on my tongue.

Nolan let out a contented sigh as he relaxed into my hold, his fingertips tightening their grip in my hair. I let my tongue stroke his, exploring his mouth like it was uncharted territory.

And in a way it was, because this kiss wasn't rushed or surprising like the last time.

It was deep, and warm, and new and I never wanted to stop. I wanted to die in that kiss on my couch, with Nolan in my arms, wearing my goddamn sweatpants.

My cock throbbed, and I groaned in response, knowing if we didn't stop now, I'd fucking own this man before he'd finished his dessert, and cold s'mores did not go down as well.

I broke away, regrettably, my gaze settling on his swollen lips, on his bright eyes and the way his lips turned up in the corners into a smile.

"But I also like *warm* s'mores, not cold ones, so let's not let my grade A baking skills go to waste, okay?" I teased.

Nolan blushed a bit as he nodded. "Yeah, yeah, of course, where are my manners?" he taunted me as he languidly reached over my fucking lap, right over my throbbing cock, to grab another delicacy.

Such a fucking brat.

He shot me a dark look as he bit into his s'more, groaning louder this time, making a show of it, if only to irritate the hell out of me.

And it worked.

"Now, be a good boy and eat your dessert and maybe I'll reward you.'

Nolan stared back at me as he took another bite, some stray marshmallow fluff spreading across his lips. I shifted my position on the couch as I reached for the last s'more, if only to hide my erection at the moment. I didn't want a repeat of last time.

No this time, I'd get it right. Because Nolan was more than a good boy.

He was fucking perfect, and I wasn't going to let him forget it.

CHAPTER TWENTY-FIVE

Nolan

I'D JUST TURNED off the faucet in the kitchen, after rinsing the plate our s'mores were served on, when Dawson spoke up.

"Come to bed with me," he said the words warmly.

I stopped drying my hands on the dishtowel. It hadn't been addressed exactly, where I would be sleeping. I'd assumed it would be the couch.

"I can sleep on the couch, it's fine."

"You are not sleeping on the couch," Dawson said, shaking his head. "That thing will kill your back and then some. You can sleep with me, my bed is more than big enough to fit us both, and I promise you, I don't bite, and I'm not going to try anything," he pledged as he held his hands up. "Unless, you want me to. But that's up to you, champ."

I couldn't help the smirk that formed on my lips. On one hand, I knew I should say no.

But something changed between us on that couch. Dawson had told me flat out he... liked me.

And then he fucking kissed me.

Thing was, I *wanted* to do exactly what he was asking. I wanted to crawl into bed with Dawson, and the last thing I wanted to do was sleep. But I was also sated from the sugar and tired from the drop in adrenaline from everything that had happened. So I really didn't have the energy to fight with him.

"Fine," I said, letting out a yawn.

"Really?" he said, a little surprised. "I thought you'd fight me on it, at least a little bit."

"Too tired to argue," I said as I sauntered over to him. "You going to show me where the magic happens or am I going to have to find it myself?" I asked as I stared up at him. Dawson's sexy grin spread wide on his face, making my entire body blush.

"Follow me, champ," he said as he turned to lead me down the hall. My heart beat loudly in my ears every step we took toward his bedroom, and that was when it hit me.

That this, sleeping with Dawson, was actually a reality, and that made me nervous.

Not because of his implications, or because of what I wanted, but because I'd literally fantasized about this moment for two years, and now that it was here, a reality, I wasn't sure what to actually do.

Fucking hell.

Dawson started to undress as we entered his room, the light coming on almost immediately.

He definitely wasn't kidding about the size of the bed. It looked big enough for three people, and suddenly the negative thoughts came rushing back. After all, he was *Mr. March,* how was I to know he didn't have orgies back at his place on the regular?

But something told me, that wasn't the case, and I decided to go with my gut instead of my self-sabotaging brain.

Just as he removed his shirt, his gaze caught mine.

"You okay, Harding?" he asked, pulling me from my thoughts. My gaze settled on him standing there, shirtless, in his damn *briefs*, looking like a five alarm fire all on his own, and my stomach twisted in knots.

"Yeah, I just..."

Dawson walked over to me, half naked without a care.

The way he stopped in front of me, how he set his palm against my cheek, thumb brushing along my jaw, fixing those golden eyes on me made me feel like I was about to become a puddle on the floor.

"Hey, I meant what I said. We don't... we don't have to do anything you aren't comfortable with. I don't expect anything from you. I want to take care of you."

The natural inclination to debunk his sweetness pestered me from inside my psyche, but I fought it.

I didn't want to ruin this moment with my anxiety and self-esteem issues. So instead of asking why, I nodded.

"Okay," I said as I let Dawson lead me to his bed like a lamb to the slaughter.

He pulled down the covers, waiting for me to get in. I curled up underneath them, in his sweatpants. I had opted not to borrow a pair of underwear, only because it felt weird to me to wear someone else's underwear—let alone underwear that belonged to the man I'd fantasized about—even if it was just a formality. I'd take my clothes to the Laundromat in the morning, hit up the local Target and get some new digs to hold me over until I could get back to my apartment and back to normal.

Dawson was definitely bigger than I was in all ways that counted, so his sweatpants were a little loose on me, but not so loose they didn't fit. They hung on my hips and I half worried they would fall down, but they seemed to hold. Though I couldn't deny that under his covers, all cozy in those sweatpants, my balls felt spoiled as all hell. The minute my back hit his mattress, I felt a wave of stress melt away.

Dawson climbed in beside me, keeping his distance and I hated it. I didn't want him to be so far away. It didn't feel right. So for once, I did what *I* wanted to do. I did what felt right, despite the voice in my head telling me otherwise. I scooted closer and threw my arm over his hip, pulling him into me.

Dawson leaned over his shoulder, looking at me.

"Really? A brat like you doesn't want to be the little spoon?"

I smirked at him in return even though he couldn't see me.

"Gotta keep you guessing or else you'll get bored," I teased him, fixing my front to his back.

The brush of his ass against my cock sent a jolt right to my damn system, and my cock immediately began to swell. A dark groan escaped my throat, which I hadn't meant to happen, but I was powerless to stop it.

I was powerless against the sex appeal of Dawson Richards.

"I don't think you'd ever bore me, Nolan," he said as he arched his back, pushing back against my budding erection.

"Fuck," I hissed as I tried to breathe through the sudden flush of heat and desire.

"I can stop if—"

"Hell no," I said as I let my hand fall

over his hip, across his stomach, my fingertips grazing the waistband of his briefs. "I like it. I don't want you to stop."

Dawson chuckled darkly as he slid his hand over top of mine, dragging it down beneath the waistband of his briefs, so I could feel his warm skin, his coarse hair, and his...

Holy fuck.

The memory of grinding myself against Dawson was still hazy, but I'd seen enough photographs of strategically placed items to formulate an idea of the size of his cock.

But the touch alone proved I had underestimated him, because it was definitely larger than what I was used to—if I was used to anything, really—and it was thicker than I'd expected.

Dawson slowly guided my hand up and down his cock, building a slow rhythm that caused my own dick to throb. Instinctively, I ground my erection against his clothed ass, just as my thumb brushed over the tip of his head to be met with warm, sticky precum, and I let out a strangled groan.

"You like that, don't you?" Dawson's voice egged me on.

"Yes," I breathed desperately.

"Is that what you want, Nolan?" His voice had taken on a hint of teasing, but it was entrenched in lust and was making my head spin.

"You want my cum down your throat, hmmm? Dripping out of your tight ass?"

Dawson thrust his cock into my fist, the wetness spreading, and I didn't think twice about what I wanted.

I slid my hand out of his briefs, and Dawson turned over, looking at me with worry.

"Yes," I said as I leaned over him, straddling his thighs again. In the low light of his bedroom, the shadows fell on him beautifully, and I tugged at his waistband.

Dawson looked up at me with surprise, but he let me pull his briefs down, and the sight of his cock springing free was better than anything I'd ever fantasized about.

As I looked at the sight of his swollen, pink cock bouncing back and forth, leaking salty, sweet precum, I wondered if I would die choking on his cock. His length and thickness alone made me half consider abandoning this plan altogether.

Maybe that wasn't such a bad way to go.

I sucked in a deep breath before signing my death certificate as I leaned down and licked his shaft from base to tip.

"Jesus Christ, Nolan!" Dawson gasped. His entire body tensed as I took him into the back of my throat in one fell swoop.

"Oh fuck!" Dawson hissed, his hands going straight for my hair. His fingers gripped my locks tight, the surprise of the moment dissipating as Dawson found himself once again. He thrust into the back of my throat, making me nearly gag. But I didn't dislike it one bit.

In fact, I kind of loved it.

"You like that, don't you?" he asked, his voice shifting to something darker. "You like choking on this dick?" He grunted as he thrust into the back of my throat again. I answered him by hollowing my cheeks, swirling my tongue around his thick head, and humming my appreciation, which only made him hiss and grab my hair tighter. So tight it hurt but in such a delicious way.

My cock throbbed in my sweatpants, and I could feel a wet spot already forming as I mindlessly thrust my own hardness against the inside of Dawson's sweatpants.

"What's the matter, champ? You all worked up with nothing to fuck?" he taunted me as he slid his cock out of my mouth, pushing forward so that I was the one now on my back, eyes wide in surprise,

Dawson's heavy, naked form held me down, his leaking cock leaving a sticky trail down my abdomen as he grabbed me by the waistband of my borrowed sweatpants.

"Dawson, please..." I begged, wanting to finish what I started. The taste of his precum still lingered in my mouth, but I wanted more. I wanted to make him come. I wanted to feel him and his thick cock bursting like a dam in my mouth. And then I wanted to—

Dawson palmed my erection through my sweatpants, right on my wet spot.

"That's what I thought," he said, his voice husky as I involuntarily thrust against his palm, feeling a mixture of shame and desire.

"Please, I need to take care of *you*," I said weakly. It was true, I did want to make him come, but it was more than that. I needed to be able to say with my body the words that were so difficult to speak with my tongue.

I want you.

I want this.

I don't want this to end...

"No, no, we're not doing that again," he said, and I wanted to ask what he meant. But before I could, he *yanked* my sweatpants down to my ankles, my own cock springing free, wet and wild.

"Look at that big, beautiful cock of yours," Dawson said, his voice all gravelly and sexy. I thrust into the air, from the sound of his voice alone. My cock literally *ached.* I wanted to come so fucking bad, and to hear Dawson like that... to see him like that... naked, swollen cock on display as he stared down at me with a startling intensity, I had to grab a hold of myself. I needed to be touched.

"Ah, ah..." Dawson growled as he smacked my hand away, the motion making my cock bounce and twinge from the impact.

"I didn't say you could do that," he teased.

"Dawson, please, I..." My words faded into nothing as Dawson's thick hardness pressed against mine and his hand wrapped around us both. The feel of his cock against mine, wet and slippery, made me see stars. A deep groan left my chest and bubbled from my lips as Dawson built a rhythm, stroking us together.

"I don't know if I can hold off. I—"

I couldn't hold it. With one squeeze and thrust, I was erupting like a damn volcano over both of our cocks, over his hand, and my vision had gone white.

"God, you are beautiful when you come," he purred as his thrusts came to a halt. "Fuuuuuck..." He groaned, long and low, the sensation of his pulsing, throbbing cock against mine throwing me into rapture. We both laid there, a sticky, wet, gross mess of mutual cum, until our breathing had returned to normal, and Dawson removed himself from atop of me, falling to the other side of the bed, his limbs still tangled with mine.

Slumber crept in under the crash of adrenaline, of relief. I vaguely registered Dawson wiping me up with a towel before crawling back into bed with me, pulling me close to him.

The last thing I remember before

darkness fell, was the warmth of his hold,
and the whisper of one word.

Mine.

CHAPTER TWENTY-SIX

Nolan

I WOKE UP to the sound of birds singing, like some damn Hallmark movie. Warmth surrounded me, and I burrowed into it like a rabbit hunkering down for winter, not wanting to open my eyes.

I wanted to hold onto the perfect, pre-awakening haze that held Dawson and I together like glue for the moment. His leg threaded through mine, his fingers cascading along my back slowly as he fought his own consciousness, no doubt.

I curled a little closer to his warm chest, the coarse, sparse hair there tickling my cheek. Pressed so close, I could hear his heartbeat, slow and steady.

I could also feel his semi-erect cock twitching against mine, and the memory of the previous night came flooding back to me, causing my own cock to wake up.

"Good Morning, beautiful." Dawson's half-asleep voice shouldn't have sounded *that* sexy, but damn if it didn't wake up every nerve ending in my body.

Instinctively, I ground my cock against him as I buried my head in his shoulder, the taut skin on his neck teasing my lips, baiting me to kiss and suck his flesh until I'd marked him like some teenage vampire.

Mine, mine, mine.

I opened my eyes, my vision blurry until Dawson's gorgeous face came into focus. I hadn't remembered taking my glasses off, but I was aware from the semi-blur of shapes behind Dawson that I didn't have them.

Which made me feel entirely more vulnerable.

That first time you spend the night with someone, where you let them see *you* underneath all that you present to the world is always nerve-wracking, but when you're letting the man of your literal dreams see you and your bedhead and your terrible vision first thing in the morning, it's something else completely.

"Morning," I said, letting out a yawn, looking up at Dawson from my spot beneath him.

"You don't have to get up," he purred, his fingertips tracing lines up and down my spine, hovering just above my bare ass.

The amount of desire that flooded me, the innate *need* to feel his fingers stretching me, was almost enough to make me come on the spot. Almost.

But I knew that despite our sexual compatibility, that if I wanted Dawson—and I did *want* him—for myself, as something more than a fulfilled fantasy, I needed to rein in my horny beast. Maybe just a little.

Not to mention there were other pressing matters I needed to attend to, that would have to be dealt with sooner rather than later. Like the claim on my apartment, getting clean clothes that fit me, and of course, calling work and Allie to let them know the details and that I was okay.

Dawson moved just slightly, hooking

his knuckle underneath my chin, forcing me to look up at him.

"I meant what I said. You can stay here as long as you need to. As long as you want... with me." His voice was still tinged with the remnants of sleep, but his words were bright and full of life.

I'd known Dawson for two years. In that time, I'd only known him to be a charismatic ass, someone who didn't seem to take things or himself seriously. But in the last several days, I'd come to see the man beneath the fireproof suit, and though he was still charismatic and a bit of an ass, he was so much more.

He was commanding, relentless, and caring.

And as I looked into his beautiful eyes, I realized that I was falling in love with him.

The absolute look of wonder in his eyes made my breath catch, rendering me speechless. No man had ever looked at me like he was looking at me at that moment. And when he leaned down, bringing his soft, warm lips to mine, I knew I was absolutely doomed.

How could I *not* fall in love with him?

Dawson kissed me, and it was better

than I'd ever imagined it could be.

He tasted like fire and love, like sweet sugar with an undercut of hot spice.

Why would I want to be anywhere else?

He broke away, too soon for my liking as he pushed away, throwing the blanket off of him.

"I however, need to get ready to head the firehouse and deal with this shit."

He grumbled as I watched his naked form saunter across the room, the sunlight casting an ethereal glow on his tanned skin. He absentmindedly tugged his sizeable cock, grunting as he did so and a part of me wanted to pull him back down into the sheets and never let him out of *my sight*.

He caught my stare, winking at me sexily, a lazy smile gracing his luscious lips.

"Be a good boy and do as you're told and maybe I'll reward you," he teased.

I sighed as I watched his bare ass leave the room, heading down the hall toward the shower. When he was gone, I fell back in the sheets, running my hand over my face.

If anyone had told me the week prior

that I'd be lying naked with Dawson's dried cum all over my stomach, I would never have believed them. But there I was in his bed, naked, hard, and ready for fucking round two.

I wanted to blame the fact I hadn't been with anyone in a couple years, and the fact that I had a real live human to touch and to touch me was the root of my sudden influx of desire, but I knew that wasn't entirely the case.

Sex for me had always been a way to communicate how I felt, when I found the words too difficult to say. And telling the guy you've been dreaming about for two years you are falling in love with him after one night in his bed screamed psycho clinger. But it was the truth.

The sound of the running shower pulled me from my thoughts. I knew I could lie there, in Dawson's bed, forever trying to work up the courage to tell him I wanted to stay, not just now but... I wanted to stay as long as he wanted me to. I wanted to be with *him* as long as he wanted to be with me. But lying there spinning myself into circles, trying to work up the nerve would only make me second-guess myself, and I wasn't about to let my self-doubt ruin this.

So instead, I threw my legs over the side of the mattress and climbed out of bed, padding down the hall to the bathroom. I gently pushed open the door, the steam in there budding like an impatient flower.

I took my time, relieving myself and washing my hands in the sink, if only to give myself the briefest moment to chicken out completely.

I knew what I wanted, but going after *anyone* was new to me. Normally, I preferred to be the one being chased, being pursued, because I'd never been a bold, confident man in any sense of the word. But something about Dawson sparked the side of me that *wanted* to be those things, that felt like maybe I could be that man with the right person.

I took one step and a deep breath as I moved toward an unsuspecting Dawson, who was humming to himself in the shower, his back to me.

Two steps, and another deep breath, and then...

I opened the curtain and quietly stepped in. Dawson turned around in surprise, his amber eyes looking me up and down with excitement and hunger. His lips turned up in a smirk.

"Nolan, what—"

"Conserve water, shower with a friend," I said, flashing him with a smirk of my own.

Dawson ran his hands through his hair, slicking the locks back as the water sluiced in rivulets down his neck.

"Of course. Think of the turtles," he said in a husky voice as I stepped closer, letting some of the water run over me.

"But if you're uncomfortable, I'll leave," I said, and I meant it. Maybe part of me was concerned I was being too forward, after all this was all new to me. Not the sex, I mean... I'd had shower sex before. But the coming onto a man like *this*... that was something I'd never done before and I had no idea what the fuck I was doing.

Dawson slid his hand over my stomach, his fingers brushing the remains of his release off of me with gentle scrubbing, before literally smacking my awakened cock. The motion made me jump as my cock bounced, twitching with desire from the rush of his rough touch.

Fuuuuck.

"You are such a fucking brat. You think you are gonna lie there in *my bed* and grind this—" He squeezed my swollen cock tightly, causing my hips to involuntarily thrust into his grasp, eliciting a groan from my mouth.

"Grind this pretty little cock all over me and then leave me hanging? Think you can crawl into this shower and tease me?" he said as he ran his thumb over my leaking hole, using his other hand to push me back against the tile. The motion angled him over top of me, and he slowly started to stroke me. My breath hitched as I relished the feel and the words of this man who held me at my wit's end.

I wanted more.

I wanted to give him *everything* I couldn't find the words to say.

"I'm not a fucking tease, Dawson, and I'm not a brat."

"Oh really? Then what are you? A good little boy? Because good boys do what they're told, and I told you to stay in bed."

Dawson let go of my cock, if only to palm his own. My gaze dipped to his thick, pink, swollen head, and I didn't think twice about dropping to my knees, staring up at him through my lashes as water rained down on me like a cleansing rain.

"If I'm so bad, why don't you teach me a lesson?" I purred, licking my lips.

Dawson smirked as he closed his position over top of me, using his hand to hold his cock as he teased my lips with the tip. Salty liquid graced my lips, and my own desire flared as I waited for him to take the bait.

I hoped by the sheer grace of God he understood that this... this wasn't about sex. It was, but it was more than that. I hoped somehow he knew that.

"Is that what you want, Nolan? You want Daddy to teach you a lesson?"

"Yes," I said, my throat going dry as my eyes fixated on his thick, engorged dick in front of me.

"Then open that pretty mouth of yours so I can wash it out with my cum," he growled, his dark eyes sparkling like hot coals, stoking the fire within me once more.

CHAPTER TWENTY-SEVEN

Dawson

NOLAN FUCKING HARDING was going to kill me.

Who would have guessed that the quiet and reserved insurance nerd would be into a little praise and degradation?

Most of the men I'd held relationships with weren't exactly into exploring that sort of power dynamic with me, not that many had gotten that far to begin with, except maybe Cade.

But Cade always had to be *guided* through the scenes, which I hadn't minded at the time, but Nolan didn't need any guidance whatsoever.

Nolan didn't miss a fucking beat. He

picked up exactly what I threw down, and he didn't even blink.

Nolan batted his pretty eyelashes at me as he opened his perfect mouth, leaning back on his heels. Water cascaded over us, and at this angle I had a clear sight of his cock, glimmering from the dewdrops of water and desire.

Everything about Nolan was absolute perfection. His dark hair, the way his glasses framed his face when he wore them, his luscious lips that begged to be stuffed with my cock, not to mention his sizeable member that was filling my brain with fuck fantasies that were less about me owning Nolan, and more about spearing myself over him and feeling *that* stretch until it hurt.

Which should have been my first clue I was in well over my head.

I wasn't bottom material. I liked to be in control, it gave me a sort of sense of purpose, of stability in my everyday life, and sex was no different. I preferred to be the one delivering the mind-shattering fucks.

But as I stared at Nolan and his beautiful cock as he sat on his heels, mouth open for me like a natural submissive, fuck if I didn't want to be owned by this man in every way that mattered.

But would he even be into that?

I pushed the thought from my mind if only because I didn't want to keep my little brat waiting for his funishment.

Not to mention, I was dying to paint his lips and face with my cum. The thought alone made me shiver as I imagined my hot spend rolling down the side of his lips.

Fucking hell, Dawson, focus or you're going to blow your load early again!

I slid my cock into Nolan's warm mouth, and he moaned a sound that made my heart swell.

"Fuuuck, your mouth feels so good..." I groaned, unable to control my words. My heart raced as Nolan grabbed my ass cheeks, pulling me closer, the angle driving my cock in over his slick tongue until I hit the back of his throat.

"That's it, fuck..." I threaded my hands through Nolan's wet locks, driving him down on my dick until I heard him gag. His face reddened under my ministrations as I fucked his mouth like I wished he'd fuck my ass.

Relentlessly.

"That's it, make me come, Nolan. Be a good boy and make me—"

The surprise touch of Nolan's fingertip as it slipped into my tight pucker made me nearly jump, but I didn't dislike it one bit.

The water ran down my skin, and the sensation of his digit pushing into me was rough and I wasn't nearly lubricated enough, but something about that made it better. I could feel every stroke, every touch tenfold as he used his one hand to fuck my hole and the other to caress my balls while he wrapped his tongue around my head.

Fucking hell, that feels amazing!

Instinctively, I picked up my pace, fucking his mouth with reckless abandon as I chased my orgasm, and the world around me shifted into a hazy blur of water, heat, and blinding release. I stilled as I gripped Nolan's hair tightly in my fists as I poured myself down his throat.

I half-expected him to gag from the amount, because even for me I knew it was a lot, but he didn't. He drank me down like I was a keg of beer, groaning like a damn porn star the entire time.

He removed his fingers from my ass, sliding them over my skin and my body went limp. When he was done, he licked the remains of my release from my tip, and then stared up at me with a sly grin on his face.

"Get up," I ordered, my breath catching in my throat. Nolan did as he was told, his gaze never leaving mine.

I wrapped my hand around his fat cock, feeling the stickiness of his excitement spreading along my fingertips.

"Good boys get rewards," I said through harsh breaths, and then I claimed his mouth with mine. Nolan startled for a moment, but relaxed against the wall, his tongue stroking mine hungrily.

I could taste myself on him, and I didn't hate it. But it wasn't what I wanted. No, I wanted to level the playing field. If Nolan was going to play dirty, I wasn't going to go down without a fight.

Nolan's eyes sparkled with fire as I squeezed him gently before dropping to my knees, an action which caused Nolan to blush redder than a tomato. Just as I knew it would.

"Dawson, wait you don't—"

I didn't wait for him to finish before I took his cock in *my* mouth, cradling his balls with one hand and stroking his shaft with the other. His entire body tensed as his eyelids fluttered closed.

"Fuck, Dawson..." he groaned. "Oh my God..." His voice was strained and that only served to egg me on more.

I moved my hand from his balls to his perineum, dragging my finger up along his seam to taunt him. I removed my mouth from his dick to look up at him and speak, using my hand to continue my strokes as I grinned wickedly.

"And you've been very good, Nolan," I said, and I happily watched his face screw up completely, once I took him back into my mouth, hollowing my cheeks as I deep-throated him.

"Oh my God, fuuuuuck!" Nolan cried in utter abandon, his cock pulsing with release as he spilled himself down my throat, fingernails scratching along the tile walls, his chest heaving with the effort to suck in stuttered breaths.

He truly was a sight to behold, and I wanted more moments like this.

I wanted all of Nolan Harding's edges and then some. I wanted to unravel him piece by piece until he was a fucking mess because of *me.*

When I was done, I rose, noticing the water had gone cold. I smiled as I leaned against Nolan, gently kissing his trembling lips. Like putty, he melted against me, and I felt on top of the world.

Nothing could ruin *this.*

"It's been fun, champ, but duty calls," I murmured, teasing his bottom lip with my teeth. I reached down and turned the now near-freezing water off.

Nolan's breaths were rapid and his pupils blown, his eyes staring at me in wonder. "Of course, don't let me stop you," he breathed heavily.

I opened the curtain, grabbing my towel as I turned to take one more look at the beautiful man in my shower, before heading to my bedroom to dress and make it to the firehouse on time.

CHAPTER TWENTY-EIGHT

Dawson

"GROUND CONTROL TO Richards!" Gina's harsh voice snapped me out of my daze. The smell of sizzling bacon invaded my airways, reminding me it was probably time to flip it.

"Don't get your panties in a bunch, Corolla," I nipped as I used the tongs to turn the bacon slices, noting that they were fairly charred at the edges.

"What is the matter with you today? I mean, don't get me wrong, you're not exactly the brightest crayon in the box on most days, but it's like you're barely tapped into Earth today."

I sighed as I flipped the burgers on the

burner next to the bacon. I'd never been the greatest cook in my own life, but at the firehouse things were different. We all took turns doing things, but somehow I'd gotten conned into being the house chef, but I didn't mind most of the time. In most ways, the firehouse was my home.

More home than my lonely apartment, anyway. Not to mention the firehouse was usually packed with my fellow firefighters on duty or coming off of it, so it was like I was always around family, which I loved. My brother was usually working, and when he wasn't, he'd make the hour and a half trek to see his girlfriend for an extended break. Since the fire though, he'd been even more scarce, hanging around if only to deal with the disaster at hand, and the minute he had an opening, he was off to spend time with the next Mrs. Bradish.

I wish I could have blamed my distraction on my brother's situation, but the truth of the matter was I couldn't stop thinking about Nolan.

About what had happened between us.

I'd been one hundred percent clear when I told him I liked him. Hell, I kissed him after that, to be one hundred percent clear... and then something crazy happened. He kissed me back and told me he liked me too, and that changed everything. The spark caught, and then ravaged us both in its flames, taking us under. And it felt *good*.

It felt more than good, actually. Being with Nolan, holding him, kissing him, tasting him... it all felt so damn right. Like that's the way it was supposed to be. And that scared me a little bit, because I'd never fallen for anyone in my life so fast before.

Sure I'd fucked on the first date before, but I'd never found myself daydreaming about being railed by any one of those guys, I can assure you.

"I'm just... tired, that's all," I lied.

Gina rolled her eyes. "I smell bullshit," she said as she opened the bag of buns, setting up the plates. The laughter from our fellow crewmembers carried from the living room, and I sighed. I didn't want to get into it all with Gina, not because I didn't trust her, but because I wasn't sure how to explain that I was falling in love with our regular claims adjuster—who I'd been more than upfront that I despised for two years.

I turned the burners off, strolling over to help Gina prepare the plates for the moment while things cooled down.

"It's not bullshit, I just—"

"Dawson, we've been working together longer than most of the assholes in this house. I know what you're like when you're tired. You don't smile from ear to ear or get a dumbass look in your eye when you need a nap. In fact, I don't think I've seen you smile like *that* since you and Cade hooked up."

She had me there.

While Cade and I had gotten off to a good start, and the sex was great, things fizzled out pretty quickly. I loved hanging out with him, and I still do, but hanging out with Cade always felt more like hanging out with my high school bestie than it did with a boyfriend. And Cade pretty much said the same thing, and we mutually agreed that being friends was probably better. But in those first few weeks, I was still riding that high of new dick, and I was pretty happy.

Did that mean that Nolan would fizzle out too?

After the haze of new dick wore off, would he get bored with me and decide we'd be better off as... friends?

God, I hoped not. To be honest, I wasn't sure if I could go back to the way things were before with Nolan, not now that I'd tasted him and let him into my heart and my bed. No, there was no way I could go back to hating Nolan, and there was no way I could just pretend he wasn't the hottest fucking nerd on the planet.

"Yeah, well... people change," I said gruffly as I laid the cheese out on the burgers.

"Whoever he is, as long as he's good to you and not an asshole—" She narrowed her eyes at me, making me feel on the spot.

"I don't know what you're talking about," I spat, even though I did.

My relationships were far and few between, but I had garnered something of a reputation for the string of *assholes* I'd collected over the years. Assholes who wanted nothing more than to get fucked by *Mr. March*, or get their firefighter fantasies out of their system.

I wasn't stupid, I knew what I was doing, and I knew those assholes weren't going to last longer than a night or two. But I wasn't looking to settle down and build a white picket fence life like Cade. I was fine with being a one night stand, or a plus one for someone's cousin's twice removed wedding.

The thought of being that now, though... where Nolan was involved, made my stomach flip.

What was happening to me?

Gina placed the pickles on top of the cheese I'd laid out.

"As long as he's good to you, treats you like a person, we're good. Because you know, that's how you *should* be treated. Not like some sex toy." She said the words quietly, which only added to their magnitude. I did know, and I hated that her words made me feel so vulnerable.

"I know," I said softly.

Gina nudged me in the shoulder. "I know you know. But you have to believe you're worth the good stuff, Dawson. Because you are."

A soft smile tugged at my lips. Gina wasn't the type to get emotional or soft. She always said things as they were, didn't mince words. Her bluntness and boldness were two of the things I loved about her and probably why I considered her my work wife above all others.

Like Cade, Gina just got me.

"I want the good stuff," I said quietly. "I just... don't know how to be the *good guy* who gets it all, you know?"

Gina and I topped the burgers with ketchup and mustard, and I felt more exposed than I had in my shower this morning with Nolan.

"What are ya waitin' for? Christmas?" Frank yelled from the living room.

Gina rolled her eyes. "We're waiting for you to grow a pair and get up off your ass and actually make yourself useful!" Gina hollered back.

It was my turn to roll my eyes, and I loaded up my arm with plates, server style.

"The natives are restless," I said with a half smile. "Come on, better get them fed before they turn to cannibalism."

Gina huffed, but she didn't argue. Instead, she followed me into the living room for another family lunch.

CHAPTER TWENTY-NINE

Dawson

IT WAS BARELY after four o'clock when I pulled up to my brother's house.

I hadn't heard anything in a couple days, and figured if I dropped by I'd know if he was home or not, and if he was, I could at least see if there was anything he needed.

Big brother habits and all.

My brother was loading his truck up.

"Headed out of town to see the misses?" I quipped as I came up to him.

"Yeah, well, it's not like I'm needed any time soon, considering that adjuster just did a re-eval of everything all over again."

"What?" I asked, confused.

Re-eval?

Nolan hadn't said anything about the claim needing to be re-evaluated.

"Yeah, apparently there was an issue, and we had to fucking start all over again. I'm just ready for my shit to be replaced, you know. Feel like these insurance assholes are just dicking me around."

My jaw tensed immediately. I wanted to believe Nolan when he said he'd make sure things were good, but it sounded like they were in fact, not good. Not at all.

Damn it!

Why didn't he say something?

I told him to keep me in the fucking loop!

I fought to keep my facial expression normal. After all, I didn't want to give my brother any more reason for alarm. I'd get to the bottom of this, and I'd take care of it.

My brother was going to get his money. I would make sure of it.

"Yeah, I know what you mean. So, uh... how long you going to be out?" I asked nonchalantly, even though my teeth ached to grind.

"Couple days. Cara has a couple days off work, so we might do a little trip up to the campground," he said with a shrug. "Get my mind off all this stupid shit, you know?"

I nodded. "Probably a good idea, I'll call you if I hear something," I said as I tapped the hood of his truck with my hand, smiling friendly enough that I hoped he bought my display.

My brother smiled in return. "Sounds good."

When I got to my car, I immediately dialed Nolan. I tried to keep my panic in check, but it was no use. Once he picked up, I snapped.

"Dawson, hey..."

"Why didn't you tell me about the re-eval?" I asked, cutting to the chase.

Immediately, Nolan turned defensive.

"What? How the hell do you know—"

"He's my brother, Nolan. It's my job to know what's going on with his life, especially when it concerns his financial stability and job."

Nolan huffed. "I told you I would take care of it, and I'm—"

"Doesn't look like you're doing a very good job," I snarled.

Nolan actually sounded a little hurt, but he snapped back, "Maybe I could do a better job if I was focused on the task at hand and not being bitched at about every move I make! I don't come to *your* job and tell you how to fight fires, Dawson. So don't sit there and act like you know one thing about what I fucking do!"

Oh the attitude on this one grinds my fucking gears.

"Why wouldn't you tell *me?* He's my brother!" I said, feeling panic racing through my veins.

"Maybe because I didn't want to stress you out, like you clearly are now," Nolan grated, his voice full of disdain and snark.

"Since when do you get to make decisions for me, huh? This is... is my life and I am the one in charge here, not you!" I spat, the words coming of their own volition.

"Whatever, Dawson. I'm not doing this with you right now. I have a *job* to do," he nipped, hanging up on me, which only served to piss me off further. I threw the phone on the passenger seat, cursing aloud in my truck.

Fuck!

The phone buzzed immediately, and I half expected it to be Nolan, but it wasn't.

It was Cade.

Just got a table, how close are you?

I closed my eyes, sighing as I remembered I had forgotten about the plans I'd made yesterday with Cade, due to the fire last night, and my morning spent under Nolan's damn spell. I tapped out my text quickly.

Be there in 10.

I only hoped maybe a good basket of cheese fries would soak up all the anger and frustration I was feeling at the moment.

CHAPTER THIRTY

Nolan

"I'M JUST GLAD you're okay, and there wasn't too much damage," Allie said, letting out a sigh.

I nodded briefly as I continued to chop the cucumbers on the cutting board for the salad I was making. While I probably should have been more pissed at Dawson than I was, a part of me was numb to people blowing up at me on the phone as I dealt with angry clients on the daily. And to be fair, until recently, I'd endured Dawson's unappreciative customer service gripes for the last two years. Dawson yelling at me didn't phase me anymore.

But what really did me in was hearing

his voice *shake* when he claimed it was his life, and he was in control. He sounded like me, or the me I was before all of this—whatever *this* was—happened.

I hated disruption, disorder. I prided myself on always doing what was right, keeping to the status quo, and keeping my nose down. I liked routine better than anyone, and I understood feeling helpless when things were out of my control.

It was just barely twenty-four hours since I'd felt that way, since I'd woken up in the middle of a literal fire and Dawson had come to *my* rescue with s'mores and sweet whispers of wanting to take care of me. So, instead of rising to his anger, instead of feeding into his need to control the situation, I did the only thing I could think of to do.

I tried to take care of *him*. Which for me, meant making my calls on the Bradish claim in between filing my own, and hitting the market to grab some stuff to make dinner.

I wasn't stupid, I knew given the situation, I'd probably be gone afterward, taking up residence at the Paradise until my apartment was ready for me to inhabit it again. So, at the very least, it was a thank you. I'd probably overstayed my welcome, anyway.

I sprinkled the cucumber wedges in the salad bowls as Allie continued.

"Still though, you have to admit it is sort of ironic that *Mr. March* came to *your* rescue like some knight in shining armor. I mean, you can't make that kind of stuff up. It's like, Hallmark material."

"It would be Hallmark material if it ended happily ever after, but we both know that's not happening."

"And why not?" Allie pressed. "I'd kill to have a hot guy make *me* dinner when I've had a shit day."

I tossed the cutting board and knife in the sink as I turned to her.

Her eyes sparkled even through Facetime, her lips smirking with smugness.

"Because that would mean I actually did something right for once," I grumbled as the timer went off for the pasta.

"You don't give yourself enough credit, Nolan. You're a damn gem, and one argument does not mean you're toast. If Dawson has any brains, he'll be groveling after tasting your damn cooking. What are you making anyway?" she said as she tried to peer around me.

I emptied the pasta into the strainer. "Chicken Alfredo and salad. Not exactly fancy, but..."

The sound of the door unlocking alerted me, and Allie's eyes widened.

"Fuck, I gotta go, Allie. I'll call you later," I said, and I hung up quickly. It wasn't like I was embarrassed or anything, but some things I liked to keep to myself. And Allie was one of those things. We'd been friends since high school, and she was the closest thing I had to a sister. I told her everything, and I mean *everything*. Something my exes didn't particularly care for.

I'd just added the cooked pasta to the sauce pot as Dawson walked through the door.

"I didn't think you'd be here," Dawson said, his entire body freezing upon the sight of me.

"Expecting someone else?" I growled, a little harsher than I'd meant to. I tossed the pasta in the pot, making sure it was coated well with sauce.

Dawson let out a sigh. "No, I just..."

"Sit down," I said briskly as I set the bowls out. A part of me worried Dawson might find my exploration of his kitchen cabinets invasive, but I hoped the scent of overpowering parmesan and bacon distracted him from the fact I'd gone through his stuff.

I had a good reason though...

I braced myself for an argument. After all, last I'd spoken to him he'd been pretty upset, and Dawson wasn't the type to take commands without a little rebuttal. I'd seen him around the firehouse. True to what he'd claimed earlier, he was usually the one in charge, telling others what to do.

So, when he did as I asked without question, sitting his ass on his barstool, eyes wide and focused on me like a kid in a candy store, I couldn't help but be surprised.

And maybe a little smug. So sue me.

"Did you actually make all this from scratch?" Dawson asked carefully.

I set the bowls of salad and pasta in front of him before sliding him a fork.

"It's the least I could do," I said as I sat across from him, focusing on my bowl of pasta because I knew if I looked at him, I'd lose my nerve.

I'd never fucking leave.

"Nolan, listen..."

I held up my hand and shook my head. "Food first. Then we can fight."

I didn't miss the small smirk that fell across Dawson's lips.

"Is that an order?" he asked, his voice edged in sarcasm.

"Just shut up and eat your damn dinner," I said, half-chuckling because he truly was a pain in the ass.

A pain in the ass that I knew I was most definitely falling in love with.

When we'd finally finished eating, Dawson moved to help me clean up.

"It's fine, I—"

"Nope, not gonna let you win this one. You cooked, I clean. Those are the rules."

I huffed in annoyance, but figured if he was in a better mood, I could let it go. It was his place after all, and I was just a guest. A guest on their way out.

"Dawson, listen... I really appreciate you letting me stay, but I think I should go. I'll grab a room at the Paradise—"

"No," Dawson said, turning to look at me with concerned eyes as he set the dishes in the sink. "Don't go on account of my being as asshole... I didn't mean, I just—"

DAWSON

Watching Dawson, a man who was usually so bold and confident, struggle over his words was somehow equally endearing as it was painful. And that melted my damn resolve, if I'd had any to begin with. I sighed.

"I was an ass. Earlier, I know I was, and I didn't mean to be, really. I just..."

I took one small step toward him, noting how his entire body *relaxed* when I did. Almost as if he really didn't want me to leave.

Dawson looked down at me with those fiery amber eyes, his gaze full of unspoken things and uncharted territory.

Full of hope.

But what did Dawson hope for?

"At the risk of sounding like an absolute idiot, I... I like you Nolan. I like you *a lot*, and I really like you being here, with me, but it's more than that..."

Suddenly, I was the one who felt like the rug had been pulled out underneath me, despite the fact I was standing on it. My throat instantly tightened, my heart skipping a beat, my blood starting to rush with the onslaught of panic and anxiety. I know what I wanted him to say, but that didn't mean he was going to say it.

Because the truth was, I liked being with Dawson too. I loved all the stupid little annoyances of his, his gorgeous face, and the little parts of him he kept hidden from most, but had decided to show me. But I knew it couldn't be *that* simple.

Could it?

"Don't get me wrong, you piss me off too. With your smug little smile, or your bratty fucking attitude, or how you can look sexier in *my* sweatpants than I do," he said, flashing me a smirk.

I was frozen as I watched his eyelashes flutter, and I waited with bated breath for him to finish. Though it sounded like he was listing my faults, which irritated me, as if I didn't already know I was a giant pain in his ass.

The feeling is mutual, though.

"But you also challenge me. Especially when *you* take control. Of the situation, of me..."

The vulnerability that crossed over his expression left my heart aching. I got the feeling that this... this soul-bearing moment was something new for Dawson, and I had to admit it was new for me too.

No man had ever looked at me like Dawson was, had ever poured their heart out to me like that. And the reality of that was scary, but also deeply fulfilling.

"Dawson..." I sighed as I took another step, noting his gaze didn't break mine. He only looked at me like I was a tall glass of water and he was in the fucking desert.

The need to soothe his rough edges, to calm his storms and insecurities was overwhelming. This man ran into burning buildings, saved people, and gave back to so much of this community.

He was a true hero, but who saved him?

Who put out the fires in his life?

Who pulled him from the wreckage?

I wanted to be that person. Dawson deserved someone who could withstand the flames, and at that moment, I found my own inner hero. I charged into his burning building, and I reached for him through the fire.

"I'd never try to control *you*. I was never trying to take that from you. I just wanted to take care of *you* for once. Take one thing off your shoulders."

Dawson reached out, and set his hand gingerly on my hip, which only made his sweatpants slide down bit.

I really need to get a pair of these in my

size, they are so comfortable...

Dawson's thumb gently brushed my exposed skin, and I'd be lying if I said the touch didn't make my entire body want to melt into a puddle on the floor.

God, I am in so deep...

Like a puppet on delicate strings, with one tiny movement of his hand, I fell into Dawson, against his chest, effortlessly.

"Damn you, Nolan," he breathed out, his other hand snaking its way up my neck and into my hair.

His touch made me feel alive, the heat of his breath on my lips, the touch of his fingertips sliding into my hair like an out of body experience. I barely had a second to breathe before his lips were on mine, warm and inviting, but not soft in the least bit.

No, there was an edge to his kiss, a roughness that caused my cock to twitch and my heart to race.

I met his harsh lips with submission, wanting nothing more than be burned by this man until there was nothing left.

Dawson pulled away only a fraction, his fingertips on my waist moving up my chest to my neck, the pad of his thumb hooking under my chin to make me look up at him. In his fiery gaze, I could see he was scared.

He was terrified of this thing between us, just as I was, and that was what I responded to as I leaned closer, biting at his lower lip, settling my hand on his hip, pulling him to me.

But inside of me there was still panic, a voice in my head that told me I was bordering on dangerous territory.

Because I wanted to give Dawson everything he deserved, everything I could possibly give the man who gives to everyone else.

But all I had to offer was me, and my racing heart.

Would that be enough?

A startling moment of clarity cut through my thoughts, and I knew I needed to take a step back. I needed to get my head on straight and think things through, away from beautiful calendar gods and addicting kisses, and pretty amber eyes.

S.O. freaking S.

"I need... I need to go," I said shakily, not wanting to leave one bit, but knowing if I didn't there would be no turning back. Because if I stayed in Dawson's kitchen, underneath his touch and kiss, I'd never recover. I would be ruined forever.

Tears threatened to escape my eyes and my heart was in my throat as I gingerly pushed away from Dawson, needing air to breathe.

Except away from Dawson, the air was suffocating.

"Please don't go, Nolan," Dawson's voice shook as his hand gently grasped mine, stopping me.

My back to him, I sucked in a breath, trying to still my racing pulse and heart as I felt the heaviness of his words.

He almost sounded heartbroken.

I was at a crossroads, torn between self-preservation and losing myself completely.

CHAPTER THIRTY-ONE

Dawson

THE FIRST DAY on the job at the firehouse, I was terrified. The training I'd endured, all the stories I'd been told, none of it would hold a candle to the first time I'd run into a burning building, nothing could truly prepare me. It was a baptism in fire, so to speak.

However, like most of those big moments in my life, I faced the fire with courage, and I refused to let my fear control me. I needed to learn how to use it to my advantage, and I had.

But that was nothing compared to the ledge I found myself on, tethered to Nolan's hand like he was a life raft, and I was in water over my head.

"Please, don't go. I... I need you." I said the words slowly, tasting them on my tongue for the first time.

I hated that I sounded so fucking desperate.

So weak.

But it was the goddamn truth, and the levity of that truth hit me like a ton of bricks as I grasped Nolan's hand. He turned to face me, and I expected to see pity, or judgment even. But that wasn't what I saw at all.

In fact, the glaze in Nolan's eyes looked as *pained* as I felt, and as if he was going to cry.

Please don't cry, champ.

"I don't want to leave, I..." His voice shook, but he took a step closer. "Why is this so fucking complicated?" he said, his voice cracking like the edges of my heart.

I took a step closer to him, feeling as if the earth beneath me was moving, shifting us toward one another like tectonic plates.

"Things don't have to be complicated, you know," I said, rubbing my thumb over the edge of his knuckles.

Nolan let out a sigh.

"They just have to be honest."

Nolan squeezed my hand tightly. The silence between us felt like an eternity until he'd spoken.

"In all honesty... I think I'm falling in love with you," he said softly, his voice barely a whisper.

My entire body softened at his words, a strange sense of relief flooding me.

I moved closer, catching his gaze. He looked as terrified as I felt, and something about that made me feel emboldened, ready to take on a new kind of fire.

The one that was spreading between us.

And I didn't want to put it out. I wanted it to consume me, consume us.

"In all honesty, Nolan... I think I fell in love with you when you beat me at that fucking race," I said as he closed the space between us.

I reached out to push his hair behind his ear, a motion that made his frames a bit crooked, but I couldn't deny it wasn't sexy.

Nolan stared up at me with glassy eyes, pouty lips, and love.

And that was all I needed.

I leaned in and kissed him, letting the

fire within my blood spread. Nolan's hands slid over my hips as his fingers dug into my sides, his lips moving slowly against mine in a torturous fashion that only made me want more.

I wanted all of Nolan fucking Harding, and I didn't care how complicated things were, or that we worked together, or that he knew how to get under my skin.

I only cared about the fact that the thought of *not* having him made me feel like I had the day I faced my first fire.

Scared.

I didn't want to lose Nolan. I'd fight like hell to keep him, and the way he touched me, kissed me, tugged at my shirt, told me he needed this too.

He needed *me* just as much as I needed him.

So, I let him pull my shirt off, let him run his hands over my muscles as I slid my hands down the waistband of *my* sweatpants he seemed to favor wearing.

I guided us through the kitchen into the hallway, the two of us hurriedly trying to undress one another as if we'd die without direct skin to skin contact.

My back slammed against the wall just outside my bedroom, pieces of clothing littered along my hallway like breadcrumbs in a forest. His lips caressed mine before moving to my jaw, and I couldn't help the groan that escaped my throat, or the involuntary thrust of my hips against his rigid cock.

"I'm sorry," I moaned into his neck, my fingertips shoving at his sweatpants and underwear.

"I'm sorry, too," he purred as his fingers quickly made a go at unlatching my belt. My cock throbbed beneath the constraining fabric, anticipating his touch.

The words that came out of my mouth belonged to me, but they were foreign to my ears. I'd never said them to anyone before.

"Guess you could say I've been a bad boy, huh, champ?" I murmured.

Nolan stopped his ministrations and looked up at me from beneath his glasses.

There was only a moment of hesitation in his eyes, before the sparkle of understanding and the spark of lust took hold.

Please punish me with that big beautiful cock of yours... Make it hurt.

"Yes, you have..." he growled, licking

his lips, his entire demeanor shifting. "You have been... very bad." He said the words as if they were another language, one he'd only just started learning.

We'll have to work on the delivery a bit.

"How bad?" I purred as I grabbed him by the hips, pulling him into my bedroom, shaking myself out of my pants. Nolan did the same, stepping out of the sweatpants, the light illuminating his cock like the true gift it was.

Nolan pushed me back against the bed, bringing his lips down to my ear. His breath on my skin was hot, causing my cock to twitch against his as he pressed himself against me.

"Bad enough I think you need to be taught a lesson," he whispered, his voice a little more comfortable.

I could feel myself starting to leak already just from the sheer magnitude of his weight, the lust in his voice... and the reality that I was giving him control in *this* situation was not lost on me.

But I trusted Nolan. I loved him, and that was all the courage I needed as I let my guard down completely.

"My safeword is ice cream," I said.

Nolan raised an eyebrow. "What?" he

asked in surprise, completely breaking character in a way that was somehow just as endearing as it was humorous.

"I don't like ice cream," I said, as if it were the most obvious thing in the world.

"You are a disgrace. Everyone likes ice cream," he chortled.

I pulled him closer as we fell back onto my bed, wrapping my leg around his hip as I thrust my cock against his.

"Just add it to my list of things you hate about me," I whispered.

Nolan smirked. "It's a long list, Dawson," he said, and he brought his lips to mine.

"Then start tallying up my punishments, baby," I breathed into his mouth.

Nolan smiled devilishly as he broke away.

"And you say I'm the one who's a brat," he teased as he stepped away, leaving me exposed on my bed.

I leaned back on my elbows, planting my feet on the edge of the bed as I stared him down. My heart thudded in my chest so loud I could hear it like an echo in the otherwise silent air.

"What are you waiting for?" I asked,

impatiently.

"To wake up from this dream any minute," he murmured as he took his palm to his cock.

I watched as he lazily stroked himself, his gaze on me heated and full of fire. "I'm waiting," I said, egging him on.

Nolan shook his head as he kneeled before me, looking as innocent as ever as he dove between my legs, taking my cock in his hand. His gaze sparkled with mischief.

"Oh, I'll teach you a thing or two about waiting, Dawson. I've waited for *this moment*, for two fucking years."

Before I could speak, Nolan took my cock into the back of his throat in one, swift motion, his tongue sliding along my shaft. Within one motion, he slid right off, and my cock throbbed, irritated to high hell that the warm mouth we'd just been in was no more.

"Fucking tease," I growled.

Nolan slid one finger in his mouth suggestively, licking and sucking as if he *wished* it were my cock, which only aggravated me. Then I watched him do the same to another finger, moaning and making a show of it as I reached for my cock, but he only used his other hand to smack me away.

Then he smacked *my* cock.

The bounce of my damn cock felt the sting, but I wanted more.

"Is that all you got?" I taunted him.

Nolan took me back in his mouth at the same time he slid one finger into my tight hole. Even though I expected the burn, it still hurt. I wasn't nearly ready enough, but I wanted it.

I wanted to be owned by Nolan, and then I wanted to own him in return.

Mine, mine, mine.

The familiar feeling of my orgasm started to swell, and I fought to thrust myself into Nolan's mouth.

"Fuck, I'm close..." I breathed out, and that's when Nolan stopped. He removed his mouth and his fingers, leaving me tingling, thrusting into the air.

Oh no...

"Good boys get rewards, Dawson. And you haven't been very good," he said haughtily as he straddled me where I lay. My cock ached, wet and ready to come.

Nolan slid his cock against mine, taking hold of both of us in his fist, squeezing. His fingertips smoothed my precum over both of our heads, and I groaned in agony. I tried to thrust, but his legs held me down.

"Please, please... I'll be good, I promise," I huffed out indignantly.

"You promise, huh?" he taunted me.

I wanted to come so bad, but I couldn't deny I was loving every minute of this.

I was loving Nolan in this role, and I didn't want to end the experience.

Nolan slid his fingers back into my hole, building a rhythm as he ground his cock against mine, making me sweat.

"Yes," I huffed. "I promise, just let me come, please..." I begged.

This feels so fucking good...

I'd never been in this position before. Usually, I was the one in charge in the bedroom and my former lovers preferred it that way, and for a long time I did too.

But there was something freeing about being at Nolan's mercy. About giving him this control over me and my body.

Which is probably why in the wild state of my lust I said what I did next.

"Fuck me," I whined like a goddamn porno.

Nolan slowed his thrusts, his eyes meeting mine with surprise.

"I mean... unless you don't want to," I said rapidly.

"Ummm... I want to, it's just... I've... never done it. Topped someone, I mean."

Of course, we probably should have had a conversation about this, but hell... Nolan and I seemed to be born in the fire.

"Well, if it makes you feel any better, champ, I've never bottomed," I said, licking my lips. "I never wanted anyone to top me, until I met you."

Nolan's eyebrows furrowed for a moment as he let go of my cock, pulling his fingers out of me, and for a minute I thought he was going to say no.

He nodded, his eyelashes fluttering as he pursed his lips.

"What if I'm no good at it?" Nolan said with a raised eyebrow.

I sat up for a moment, pulling him between my legs, letting my fingers trace over the flesh of his ass, of his seam.

"I think you'll be *very good*, Nolan," I said softly. "Just channel all that hate and waiting and I think you'll be just fine." His cock was right at my mouth level, so I didn't waste the chance to lick the salty liquid gleaming at his slit. I enjoyed watching his entire body shudder.

"Okay..." he said as he took a breath, his eyelids falling shut from my tongue swipe for a moment before he opened them, peering at me with a boldness that only made me want his fury more.

"Lube?" he asked, his voice bolder.

I sucked at the head of his cock before answering, eliciting a tiny whimper from him.

"Top drawer," I responded, before taking his entire cock in my mouth.

Nolan pulled back, the sound of the cap popping echoing in the room.

"Okay, lean back," he instructed methodically.

I obeyed without question, my nerves starting to circulate as reality hit. Right before two cold, wet fingers wedged themselves in my hole again, this time sliding in with ease as they built a rhythm. My head fell back instantly as ecstasy coursed through me, and then Nolan slid a third finger in. The stretch was good, but I needed more.

I needed Nolan and his big, beautiful cock to fucking own me.

"Are you ready?" he asked, his voice full of desire and anxiety.

I nodded, my eyes closing in ecstasy.

"Yes," I said. "Teach me a goddamn lesson, Nolan."

There was a brief moment where I thought he might have reconsidered, but when I felt the tip of his cock pressing against my slick entrance, nothing else mattered.

He took it slow, inch by inch and the stretch felt fucking amazing. And then he slid in the last few inches and my insides *clutched* him like a vice. A deep groan escaped both of us, and immediately Nolan's head buried itself into my shoulder.

"Fuck that feels good," he whined. "*You* feel really good."

I slid my legs around his hips, the motion driving him in deeper.

"*You* feel really good, champ," I said through my teeth, and I fucking meant it.

I felt so fucking full.

Of excitement, of relief, of love... and cock.

Nolan's chest rose and fell against mine as he gently bucked his hips, the movement shooting pleasure through my damn spine. I needed more. I was so freaking close to coming.

"Look at me," I ordered, sliding my hands in Nolan's silky locks. He followed my touch as I turned his head toward me.

Nolan rocked his hips into me a little faster, and I lost myself in the feel of him filling me to the brim, the weight of his body on mine, and the way he was looking at me.

The words fell out of my mouth of their own volition.

"I love you," I said, my cock sliding against his abs torturously, leaving sticky trails on his skin.

Nolan leaned down and took my lips like a damn prayer.

"I love you too, asshole," he whispered, both of us toppling over the edge into ecstasy. His thrusts halted as warmth spread within me, his hot release filling me and spilling out of me as he drove his tongue down my throat.

My cock pulsed as I came hard and fast against his abdomen, painting his skin in my sweet release.

I wrapped my arms around Nolan and held onto him for dear life as we came together like a well-oiled machine.

And when we'd finally disconnected, I'd never felt more whole.

CHAPTER THIRTY-TWO

Nolan

"YOU DON'T HAVE to get up," Dawson whispered in my ear, tugging me closer to his chest.

I guess I didn't mind being the little spoon once in a while...

I groaned as I grabbed his hand, threading my fingers through his as I tried to hold on to sleep.

"Yes, I do. I have a bunch of stuff to catch up on at work," I whined.

Dawson kissed me below my ear, before nibbling on the bottom of my earlobe like a starving man. The feel of his tongue and teeth on the sensitive skin there gave me goosebumps and ignited my fire, but I knew neither of us had time to waste.

It had been a week since we had unofficially-officially sealed the deal. One week since Dawson and I had been honest about our feelings. One week since I'd been staying with Dawson while my apartment was being renovated, and one week since I'd submitted paperwork along with the Bradish re-eval to my higher ups in an escalated claim.

While Karla had given me the option to take a few days regarding my fire situation, I hadn't taken her up on the offer. I knew I'd need to get to work sooner or later.

Regrettably, I broke Dawson's hold, and we both did the adult thing and got our asses moving. I made breakfast while Dawson showered, then took my turn when he was out. I'd just started buttoning up my last button when Dawson stopped me.

"What?" I asked, noting the look of mischief in his eyes.

"Your glasses are crooked," he said, flashing me a smirk.

"What?" I asked as he reached out to adjust them, the motion putting his fingers above my ear, giving him access to slide them into my hair and pull me close.

I wasn't sure I'd ever get used to being *loved* by Dawson.

I'd been used to being tormented and pissed off by Dawson, but being loved by him far outweighed everything else.

It was a feeling I hoped I'd never lose.

"Personally, I like it. But, we can't have you looking like you just rolled in the hay with *Mr. March* when you walk into work,"

"Mhmmm. But you can walk into work with a hickey on your neck and no one says a word?"

Dawson blushed as he craned his neck, the faint markings still visible after a few days.

"Oh, they'll say words. And I'll tell them all the sordid details if they do ask," he said, grinning ear to ear.

I twisted my lips. "That sounds like very bad behavior," I teased him.

"The worst. Definitely worthy of punishment, if you ask me."

I shook my head in defeat. There was no use fighting Dawson when he'd made his mind up about something, and that something was me.

Or more accurately, my form of

discipline.

But I wasn't complaining. I was more than happy to explore this new side of me, and Dawson seemed to enjoy reaping the benefits.

And he also had no problem putting me in my place either.

"I'll take that into consideration," I said, and I pressed my lips to his.

"You still good for M's Place later?" he asked as he finished my last button.

"Yeah, good as I'm going to be, I guess," I answered honestly.

It felt stupid to hide the fact we were together anymore, and neither of us wanted to feed the gossip mill, so we'd decided to be upfront and honest with everyone that mattered. Our jobs, and our friends.

I'd officially be meeting Dawson's friends tonight, as his boyfriend, which still baffled my mind.

Hearing him call me that made me blush, made my heart race, and my lips turn up in a smile.

Because the way he said it was like I was the fucking sun.

My boyfriend.

The feeling was more than mutual.

CHAPTER THIRTY-THREE

Nolan

"THAT SHOULD JUST about do it," I said as I shook Jonathan Bradish's hand, just as I heard the rumblings of Dawson's truck.

"I really appreciate everything you've done, Mr. Harding," Jonathan said with a sigh of relief. "This check is going to take care of a lot of stuff and then some," he said appreciatively.

"Please, you can call me Nolan."

That was the moment Dawson walked in.

"Everything okay?" Dawson asked as he looked between us.

Jonathan smiled. "Better than okay.

Mr. Harding here went above and beyond," Jonathan said with a chuckle.

"Is that so?" Dawson said, raising an eyebrow at me.

"Because of the error in the initial report, not to mention the initial findings—" I raised an eyebrow back at Dawson, who only sheepishly blushed. "I was able to file a complaint along with my re-eval and I escalated the claim above my supervisor so it would get pushed through faster, being as there were extenuating circumstances and someone's livelihood at stake." I smiled smugly.

"Breisinger cut me a check for thirty grand, Daw," Jonathan said grinning ear to ear.

"Thirty grand? That's... that's more than—"

"It's what he deserves. This place is his business, after all," I said firmly.

Dawson didn't waste a second. He swooped in and hugged me tight, then *kissed* me with such appreciation I found it hard not to wrap my arms around him and do the same.

When we broke apart, his brother was shaking his head.

"I should have known," he said as I

fought to regain myself, steadying my blush and my glasses, which had gone crooked from Dawson's prince charming moment.

"What do you mean?" Dawson asked, clearing his throat, casting me a sly grin.

"I mean, the tension between you two when you last showed up here was thicker than a fucking poundcake."

We both laughed, and I could see I was not the only one blushing.

"That obvious, huh?" Dawson asked with a chuckle.

His brother rolled his eyes. "Well that, and you've been talking about the guy for like, two years."

I turned to raise an eyebrow at Dawson. "Really now? I hope they were only good things," I teased him.

Dawson grinned devilishly.

"Actually they were terrible things. Long list of grievances."

I bet they were.

"Mhmmm." I fought my own smile as Dawson wrapped his arm around my shoulder and pulled me tightly to him, pressing his lips to my forehead.

EPILOGUE

Dawson

"IF I RECALL correctly, I believe your words were, 'not if he was the last dick on earth,'" Mitchell said with a grin.

Nolan turned to look at me with judgment. "Really, Dawson?"

"To be fair, you were quite infuriating..." I scoffed.

Nolan rolled his eyes. "Says the asshole whose sole desire in life was to make my job a living hell."

"Maybe that wasn't his only desire," Cade said with a smirk.

"Obviously," Weston chimed in as he pulled Cade close.

"I'm surrounded by idiots," I huffed,

throwing my hands up in the air.

The waiter came with our drinks and a basket of wings, and I noticed someone kicking me under the table. I didn't have to look to know who it was, since it was coming from the seat beside me. I shot a wary look to Nolan, who was smugly shaking his head.

"You are an idiot," Nolan teased.

"But you still love me," I teased him back.

Nolan shook his head.

I licked my lips as I dove in for a wing as the karaoke singer exited the stage.

"Don't worry you can get your revenge later," I said, flashing him a wink as I ate my wing.

"I'll hold you to that," Nolan promised, taking a sip of his beer.

"I'm counting on it," I growled wickedly as I leaned in and kissed the man of my damn dreams quickly in front of all my friends, in the glow of the bar where it all started.

The karaoke singer who'd taken the stage actually sounded really good, singing Ozzy's *Bark At The Moon*.

"I'm going up," Nolan said as he jumped off the barstool beside me.

"Really now? Since when do you like being the center of attention?" I scoffed.

Nolan stood straighter, adjusting his glasses and looking at me with that bratty cockiness I'd come to fucking love about him. He may have been hot as hell when he was in charge, but God Almighty did I love it when he turned on his brat charm.

I wasn't sure what I liked more, to be honest, stuffing my cock down Nolan's throat to teach him a lesson, or him edging me and fucking me into oblivion.

He placed a hand on his hip and with the utmost attitude said, "You can't stop me." And like the little pain in the ass he was, he stuck his tongue out for good measure.

As if he trusted I wouldn't bend his ass over my damn lap and smack it right here.

Pain in my ass.

"Oh yeah?" I asked as I left my wings and beer and sauntered over to him, holding him in my stern gaze.

"Yeah," he taunted me.

I grabbed him by the waist, pulling him to me. His eyes widened in surprise for a moment, but his body melted in my hold like butter.

Nolan slid his hands in my hair, staring up at me with bright eyes from behind crooked glasses.

I set my palm against his neck, using my thumb to tilt his chin up, and took his lips against mine without warning. I could taste the hint of hopps on his tongue, and just like all the other times, he fell into my hold with ease, groaning as I coaxed his tongue with mine. I was aware my friends were hollering and bitching at us to get a room, but I didn't care. It was all in good fun anyway.

Nolan broke apart from me for a moment, and I watched the blush creep over his nose and cheeks, relishing in the way his glasses had gone crooked from our kiss.

"You'll pay for that," he whispered, his voice full of lust, his cock twitching against mine.

"I'm counting on it, champ," I said as the fire in Nolan's eyes shifted, and he took charge, and kissed *me*, making all my wildest dreams come true.

Thank you for reading Dawson and Nolan's story.

If you enjoyed this book, please return to your favorite retailer and leave a review. Even a few words could mean the world to an author.

Continue the series with Drew's story, Book 3 in Jasper Springs!

OTHER BOOKS BY EVIE

Federal Protection Agency
Mason
Rafe
Ryzen
Cooper
Noah
Damien
Sebastian
Gabe
Logan

Ruthless Empire
Courting Danger
Chasing Danger
Kissing Danger

Smokejumpers
Hawke
Cyrus
Jase
Gage
Jackson
Xavier

Jasper Springs
Cade
Dawson
Drew
Grayson
Riley
Mitch

From The Edge
Shattered
Runaway
Jaded
Rescue
Hidden
Tormented

Gray Vale Pack
His Fated Mate
His Wounded Warrior
His Healing Heart

ABOUT THE AUTHOR

Evie Riley is a prolific, neurodivergent author known for her captivating MM romance novels. She has gained a significant following and topped the LGBT+ action and adventure bestseller charts with her series.

Evie's writing style often explores dark and gritty themes where her men must overcome difficult obstacles in their search for love, but she has also ventured into sweeter small-town romances, incorporating tropes like enemies-to-lovers, friends-to-lovers, age-gap, and forced proximity. She is known for crafting engaging romantic suspense novels and has a knack for creating interconnected series worlds that keep readers invested.

EVIE RILEY

Interestingly, Ms. Riley has hinted at exploring new genres, such as Alien Omegaverse Romance, in the future.

Outside of writing, she enjoys spending time at the beach and has a quirky personality, described by her partner as ranging from cute to deadly, depending on her blood-chocolate levels.

Evie spends her nights writing bad boys in love, and her days wrangling the sweet boys she loves.